A Fear of Heights

From here, it is a short distance to the insignificant summit of Brandreth, and down into the mist again to a broad eroded track to Great Gable where the path swoops dramatically to a narrow saddle and then rises steeply to the main summit. The scrambling requires care, but Jim is right, it is not difficult. He waits for her, and Tamsin finds herself enjoying the sensations of quickly gaining height, reaching, stretching, pausing to see the route ahead up a zigzag cairned path. She is doing it: she is climbing and is not afraid, even when she looks down to the sunlit slopes far below her feet; she feels fit and capable, following Jim's sure lead. The gradient lessens towards the mountain's bouldery summit. Jim waits for Tamsin as she mounts the last few yards, and throws his arms round her as she comes to meet him.

A FEAR OF HEIGHTS

Linda Newbery

Collins

An Imprint of HarperCollinsPublishers

Summer and Spring (part VIII of *A Man Young and Old*) by W.B. Yeats is reproduced by kind permission of A.P. Watt Ltd on behalf of Michael Yeats.

First published in Great Britain by
Collins in 1995

Collins is an imprint of
HarperCollins*Publishers* Ltd,
77-85 Fulham Palace Road,
Hammersmith, London W6 8JB

1 3 5 7 9 8 6 4 2

ISBN 0 00 674766-3

Printed and bound in Great Britain
by HarperCollins Manufacturing Ltd, Glasgow

With thanks to Ann-Janine,
for constructive criticism;
to Rod, Carol and Charlotte, for technical detail;
to Roger, for reconnaissance;
and to Trevor, for tolerance.

CONTENTS

PERSONAL COLUMN

*T*amsin doesn't want to start packing. Once she gets her bags out and puts them on the bed, it will seem as if she doesn't live here any more. It won't be like packing for a holiday; more like packing up her whole life. She imagines herself as a parcel in transit for the next few days, neither really here nor really there. Sitting cross-legged on the floor of her room, she delays taking things from shelves, drawers and wardrobe by fiddling with her list, adding items, crossing others off, doodling round the edges. She wonders why, instead of the excitement she expected, she feels only reluctance.

Her mother's feet clomp up the wooden stairs to Tamsin's attic room and she appears in the doorway.

"How are you getting on?"

"Still only thinking about it," Tamsin says.

Her mother sits on a low cushioned stool, removing Tamsin's teddy bear, which she puts on her lap. "Here. Have a look at this." She hands Tamsin a notepad with a few lines written in bold capitals.

Tamsin looks. "Mum! You're really going ahead with it then?"

"Why not?" Abigail says defensively. "It's worth a try. There's no commitment."

Tamsin reads aloud: "SINGLE MOTHER, 37, INTERESTED IN PAINTING, PHOTOGRAPHY AND THE CINEMA, SEEKS CONSIDERATE MAN FOR COMPANIONSHIP AND OUTINGS." She wonders whether Abigail would have kept the whole thing secret if it hadn't been for her own accidental discovery of last Saturday's *Independent*, folded back at the personal columns with some of the entries ringed round. Confronted, Abigail admitted that she was considering placing an advertisement of her own.

Until now, if Tamsin had thought about Lonely Hearts advertisements at all, she would have considered them to be the last resort of people who were desperate, painfully shy or socially inept, or, on the other hand, a bit of a joke for brash young career people in search of a good time. Not for mothers. Not for *her* mother. Although Abigail is treating it lightly, Tamsin realises that she must be lonely, or fears being lonely now that she will be living by herself for the first time in eighteen years.

"What do you think?" Abigail asks. "Will it do?"

Tamsin reads the wording again, silently. She is not at all sure that she likes the idea of her mother being advertised like an item of livestock. What sort of person would be attracted? Since hearing of her mother's decision, and because she really can't think of any reason why Abigail shouldn't be entitled to meet people of the opposite sex, Tamsin has made a careful study of the *Independent* advertisements. The rows of closely printed type begin to frame characters, stories. LIVELY, AFFECTIONATE WOMAN, EARLY FORTIES, GOOD SENSE OF HUMOUR, WISHES TO REBUILD LIFE AFTER BROKEN MARRIAGE, read one. ARE YOU THE WOMAN I'VE BEEN LOOKING FOR ALL MY LIFE? pleaded another. Everyone, it seems, has a good sense of humour, is lively, energetic, warm, loving, in various combinations. Why are there so many successful, well-balanced people, all in search of that most elusive kind of fulfilment, Tamsin wonders.

But her study has a more immediate purpose – she is worried that her mother doesn't know how to behave with strange men. Clearly, this sort of thing must be approached carefully. There are no phone numbers, for obvious reasons; box numbers instead, for anonymity. Some of the entries sound conceited enough to put off anyone sane at a first reading. Others sound mild and modest enough, but she wonders what predatory instincts lie beneath the careful wording. She doesn't like the thought of her mother risking contact with strangers.

She frowns at the handwritten draft. In spite of her uneasiness at the idea of her mother packaging herself for potential male interest, she thinks the wording is unduly modest.

"Shouldn't you say *attractive* single mother?" she points out.

Abigail looks doubtful. "It sounds so vain to say it about yourself. It might put people off, or make them expect someone who looks like Michelle Pfeiffer."

"Lots of the *Independent* ads say it. Anyway, it's true in your case, more than for most of them, I bet. And if you don't say it, they'll think you're hideous."

"No, leave it as it is," Abigail says, and takes the notepad back. "What about the rest?"

Tamsin considers. "I'm not sure about 'single mother', either. People might think you've got a baby or a two-year-old who's going to get in the way. You could say 'teenage daughter', or 'daughter at university'."

Abigail chews her lower lip thoughtfully. "That's as good as announcing that I was a teenage mother. It'll raise questions."

"Yes, but at least they'll know you're not going to have baby-sitter problems, or be cluttered up with pushchairs and nappies. Or perhaps you don't need to mention that you're a mother at all."

"It might be as well to let them be put off, if they don't like the idea of families." Abigail straightens the teddy bear's droopy bow-tie. "It's a way of weeding out the non-starters."

Tamsin recalls the precise specifications in some of the adverts she has read. "What about age? – not yours, theirs. They usually give a range for what they want. What sort of age *do* you want?"

"Oh, I don't know," Abigail says vaguely. "It doesn't matter much, does it?"

Tamsin thinks it might matter quite a lot. After all, Mum wouldn't want a twenty-year-old toy boy – would she? – nor an overweight retired businessman. Really, she considers it ridiculous that her mother should feel it necessary to advertise for a . . . she doesn't even know what term to use. Boyfriend? That sounds too young, or too coy. Companion? Too cosy and platonic. Lover? Too blunt, and it conjures visions which Tamsin does not want to entertain. Gentleman friend? No, that sounds like a Victorian euphemism. Tamsin gives up. She doesn't know why someone as youthful and outgoing as her mother should find it difficult to meet suitable men. "You're lucky to have such a young mum," Tamsin's friend Becky often says, after a dispute with hers about curfew hours. Becky's mum is a good ten or fifteen years older than Tamsin's: plump, with greying hair, determinedly making the most of her declining attractiveness by wearing bright colours and bizarre earrings. She appears to be a generation further on than Abigail, who is sometimes mistaken by strangers for Tamsin's older sister. Abigail's thick chestnut hair, the same colour as Tamsin's, has recently been cut most becomingly in a wavy bobbed style; she has a slim figure and an oval face which Tamsin considers quite beautiful.

"Finding the right sort of person is difficult," her mother has explained. "At my age I'm not going to hang around bars and parties. I need to meet someone with similar interests."

"Isn't there anyone at the art club?" Tamsin suggested. "That would be the ideal way to get to know someone."

"Oh, there are some nice people there," Abigail said evasively, "but I know them all too well. That's the problem."

Tamsin accepts the explanation but cannot shift her feelings of unease about the whole idea. Especially as she will be packed up and gone by the day after tomorrow. She doesn't begrudge her mother the chance for fun and romance, if that's what the advertisement can provide; it might even help to assuage some of her own guilt about leaving Abigail on her own. But she hates the thought of being far away, out of reach, not knowing where her mother is or who she is seeing. You never know who might be reading the personal columns, and with what motive in mind.

"Mum, you will be careful, won't you?" she says now, picturing dark streets and shady alleyways. "I mean, meeting these people for the first time – how are you going to do it? It might not be *safe*."

Abigail pushes her hair back and smiles. "Don't worry. It ought to be me worrying about what *you* might get up to. Leaving the nest and all that."

"I'll be all right," Tamsin says.

"Yes, I know you will. You've always known what you want to do and now you're doing it. You're far more sensible than I was at your age."

Tamsin looks away, a little embarrassed. She isn't sure that she really is quite as sensible as her mother imagines. Admittedly, she isn't about to run away with her boyfriend and get pregnant, which is what Abigail did at eighteen, but there are other ways of being less than sensible.

"Anyway, don't change the subject," she persists. "About meeting these men . . ."

"It's all right. I've read articles about it. There are sort of rules. You don't go round to people's houses or let them come to yours, obviously, not until you feel you know them. First you have a conversation on the phone, and if you decide he's all right then you arrange to meet at a pub, or somewhere like that where there are other people about."

"Well, be careful!"

Tamsin can't shake off the absurd feeling that she ought to go along as a chaperone. Mum isn't a sixteen-year-old going on her first date, for goodness' sake. It isn't as if she's never had relationships with men. There have been two fairly long-term attachments: Bill, long ago when Tamsin was still in primary school, who seemed like a big friendly dog around the house, and more recently Gavin, who Tamsin never really trusted. She was right, too: his relationship with Mum was an on-off one, with hissed rows over the telephone, frequent dramatic walkings-out and then walkings-back-in-again. Cuddly Bill went to live in Australia; Gavin made his final exit two years ago, ending Tamsin's speculation that she could end up with a step-brother and two step-sisters if he and Mum ever stopped arguing for long enough to get married. She was just beginning to think that she might like being part of a proper family, even one with Gavin in it, when Mum decided she'd been messed about for long enough. And for the last couple of years there hasn't been anyone at all, Abigail devoting herself to painting, with considerable local success.

"Here goes, then. I've changed it a bit. SINGLE WOMAN, 37, DAUGHTER AT UNIVERSITY, and the rest's the same as before. I'll send it off tomorrow. It won't be printed until Saturday week and by the time any replies come I'll be back from Claudia's." Abigail looks round at the untouched room. "You don't seem to have done any packing at all."

"I know. I'm just looking at my list and wondering what I've forgotten."

"Want a hand?"

"Not at the moment, thanks. I'm not organised enough yet."

"I'll start cooking then. Ready to eat in about half an hour?"

"OK."

Abigail's sandalled feet clomp downstairs. Tamsin stands up, stretching, and then remembers that she hasn't put *contact lens container* or *rinsing solutions* on her list of things to take; the contact lenses are a new investment, and she hasn't got used to the routines yet. She writes quickly, wondering whether Becky is doing her packing too. Becky will be going to a London college, near enough to come back for weekends; she wants to be near her boyfriend, Greg. Tamsin thinks this is probably a mistake. People grow up and change during those important college years; it seems a pity to tie yourself down from the start. She doesn't intend to, not now, not for a good many years, if ever. She doesn't expect to meet a man who is worth it.

Becky's grades weren't as good as she hoped, and she had to trawl round after the results came out to get a place at all. Tamsin, who got her first choice with grades to spare, was glad when it was all settled. Becky would have been dreadfully upset if she'd had to resit her A-levels, or give up the idea of university altogether. But their four-year friendship is about to be disrupted, as they both know.

"You'll be *miles* away," Becky exclaimed when

Tamsin's place was confirmed and they sat together in Becky's garden looking at the road atlas. "Right up there near Manchester and Sheffield. Why do you want to go so far away?"

"Typical Southerner, aren't you?" Tamsin teased. "Anywhere north of Watford Gap and you think it's the Arctic Circle. I *wanted* to go somewhere different, not just round the corner. That's part of going to university."

"But we won't see each other," Becky said. "Not unless I end up having to take a place at Sheffield or John o' Groats or somewhere."

"We'll both be home again at Christmas," Tamsin said. "The terms aren't that long. And there's always Greg."

"Oh, yes," Becky said in a gooey way that made Tamsin feel sick.

Their friendship has already changed over the past eighteen months or so, since Becky has become so inextricably involved with Greg. Tamsin teases Becky for being soppy and sentimental, part of a cosy twosome; Becky accuses Tamsin of being a swot and a man-hater.

"The way you *dress*. Anyone would think you wanted to look as drab and bookish as you possibly can. You'd look really attractive if you tried a bit harder. Your mum's trendier than you are!"

"I don't care much about what I wear, that's all," Tamsin protested. "And I don't hate men! Some of them are quite pleasant. But I don't need one of my own. Not yet."

"Well, don't wait too long. With anyone else, I'd have thought they'd chosen Engineering because they'd be outnumbered about forty to one. But I bet that's never even crossed your mind."

"It's not forty to one. Women engineering students are about fifteen per cent, and going up. Anyway, I don't mind being outnumbered by males. I can have interesting conversations with them about welding and stresses."

Tamsin knows that as far as Becky is concerned, an engineer is someone in greasy overalls, wielding a spanner underneath a lorry. No amount of explanation or showing Becky the prospectuses can change that.

But Tamsin is less confident than she sounds, especially now, on the brink of departure. The future is vague, full of the shadows of unmet people, while those she loves will be out of reach. Mum needs her, and then there's Nan, who has recently been ill; they have always been a close family, and perhaps she is being selfish to make such a drastic change. Perhaps it would have been better to apply to a college nearer home, after all. Tamsin gazes round her room at all the things she can't take with her but doesn't want to leave behind. Edward, her ancient teddy bear, is sitting on the stool where Abigail left him. You *can't* take a teddy bear with you, she tells herself; he'll have to stay behind. She still thinks of her teddy as *he*, even though, as from Friday, she's going to be an undergraduate scientist. She doesn't feel much like an undergraduate, nor a scientist for that matter.

What if she finds the course too difficult? What if she fails the first-year exams? Her high A-level grades give little reassurance: the hurdles ahead are going to be higher and more difficult. She feels no confidence at all. She finds it amazing that everyone, Mum included, sees her as the embodiment of efficiency and maturity when such whirlpools of self-doubt churn inside. Is it so easy to fool people?

She looks at the painting on the wall opposite. It is one of her mother's most recent: two figures in a garden, painted in bright early-summer colours, so that the foliage and flowers and the azure-blue of the woman's dress seem to float in space, above purply shadows cast by shrubs in the foreground. Abigail's sense of colour often strikes Tamsin as unusual but just right, a heightening and intensification of something half-perceived in nature. It has taken years for her own distinctive style to evolve, but now she has found it, and paints fluently and purposefully as if all her best work was waiting for this flowering of talent. Tamsin can sense her mother's intense satisfaction, even excitement, when she is working on a picture and it starts to take shape as she wants. Abigail drifts about the house with a peculiarly rapt, inward-looking expression, during which phase Tamsin knows better than to expect normal conversation or adherence to domestic routines. Practicality is not her mother's strong point.

Artistic ability appears in alternate generations of the family. Tamsin's great-grandfather survives through his paintings, one of which hangs in Abigail's bedroom. The gift skipped over Tamsin's Nan, resurfaced in Mum, but shows no sign of emerging in Tamsin. She is interested in her mother's work and likes to visit exhibitions but has little flair herself, dropping art at school in favour of extra science.

Soon after that she decided to study engineering. Although good at most school subjects except games, she has always excelled at science, an inclination which her mother claims was passed down from Grandad Charlie. Tamsin is more curious about the characteristics she has inherited from her own father, who is a complete stranger. Abigail was a single parent before the term was fashionable. Teachers at parents' evenings always wanted to call her Mrs Fox, but she wouldn't let them. "It's *Ms* Fox," she would say firmly, leaving the staff to speculate whether she meant Ms as in I'm-not-giving-away-my-marital-status-every-time-I-use-my-name, or Ms as in Miss, which is what some people still take it to mean. Tamsin was embarrassed by it at primary school, having a mother who wasn't called Mrs, but now she shares her mother's point of view. Why should Abigail pretend to be Mrs for the sake of convention, when she's never been married?

* * *

When she was much younger, Tamsin found her family relationships difficult to understand. There was a marked absence of fathers. Mum had one, but nobody else did.

The old painting in Mum's bedroom had something to do with it. "The green lady", Tamsin called it, because its real name was something Irish which she couldn't pronounce. She liked all the soft pretty things in Mum's room, the embroidered pattern on the duvet, the nightdress folded under a pillow, the sweet-smelling bottles and jars which she touched but did not open. She liked to scramble up on the bed and huddle there with her knees and toes sinking into the duvet, looking up at the green lady who smiled sadly and wore a draped robe. Tamsin liked to find the pictures behind the green lady, half-hidden in a mist: a big running dog, mountains, rivers, people fighting.

"It's the story of Ireland," Mum would say, sitting sideways on the bed, coming to look at the picture too as if she could always find something new there. "Your great-grandfather painted it. He was Irish."

Tamsin didn't understand who her great-grandfather was. She had a grandad, Grandad Charlie, who was quite old, so her great-grandfather must be very very old; she pictured him with a long white beard and a walking-stick. Why didn't he ever come to see her? And then once at Nan's, Nan had shown her another picture, of a man who was smiling in a sad way rather like the green lady. She said, "This is your great-grandfather." Tamsin didn't think that could be right. Her great-grandfather wasn't very old at all, only about Mum's age.

Later she understood that her great-grandfather had died in Ireland soon after painting the two pictures. He was Nan's father, but he had died before she was born.

"That's the same as mine," Tamsin said.

"No," Mum corrected. "Your father isn't dead. He and I don't live together, that's all."

Tamsin was very puzzled about fathers. Most people had them; Tamsin knew what fathers were, but for some reason she and Nan weren't allowed to have one. Theirs had been taken away.

Something else worried her as well.

"How can that man be Nan's father,' she asked, "if he died before Nan was even born? I can't see how he had anything to do with her."

Mum tried to explain, but Tamsin remained convinced that there must be some mistake.

Somewhere, there is a thirty-eight-year-old man called Paul Strivener who is her father.

When she thinks about him, which is increasingly often, Tamsin sees him as a shadowy shape behind her, a blank form without features. Her mother is not forthcoming on the subject. "He was an idle waster," she says, if she can be persuaded to say anything at all, or, "He was totally unreliable." Tamsin can understand her reticence; Paul Strivener abandoned her when she became pregnant at the age of eighteen, and they haven't met since. Tamsin has never been able to get much information out of her; the more she tries, the more her mother clams up. Only once has Abigail spoken seriously about what happened, usually hiding her feelings in either flippancy or silence. But the fact remains that Paul Strivener does exist; he has given Tamsin half of what she is. Sometimes she looks in the mirror, wondering. Her hair colour obviously comes from Mum, but Tamsin's eyes are greyer than her mother's clear blue, and her face is thinner, her cheekbones more pronounced and her nose straighter than Abigail's. Some of that must have come from Paul Strivener.

Does he ever think about her? Wonder what she looks like, what she's doing? She wishes she could meet him. She can't go through her whole life without finding out more about him.

"Your mum will have to agree to it," Becky always says. "It's your right to know. I'd be eaten up with curiosity."

"Well, so am I. I want to see him, even if it's only once. I don't expect to *like* him – I couldn't possibly. I don't even want him to see me."

"What are you going to do, turn yourself into the Invisible Woman?" Becky joked.

"Well, it'd be embarrassing, wouldn't it, coming face to face? After all, he could hardly pretend that he's ever shown any interest in me or Mum. I was just an accident – he couldn't wait to clear off. But I still want to know what he's like. It's quite likely I've got half-brothers and sisters I don't even know about."

"You might pass him in the street every day and neither of you would be any the wiser," Becky said. "Have you thought of that?"

"I've thought of all sorts of things. But Mum told me once that he'd moved to the north-east, Cleveland or somewhere, the last she heard."

A few months ago, Tamsin decided that on her eighteenth birthday she would tell Abigail that she wanted to find out where her father was, and meet him. But when her birthday came in early June, right in the middle of A-levels, there was a scare about Nan: she was taken into hospital with acute stomach pains, and it was altogether the wrong time for Tamsin to give her mother anything else to worry about. Nan made a good recovery after a few weeks and seems as fit as ever, but still the subject remains unbroached. Sometimes Tamsin thinks that half of her doesn't want to know any more about her father, in case she doesn't like what she finds out.

FRESHERS

*T*amsin thought her own pile of belongings was on the large side, especially when she and her mother tried to cram it all into the car, but on arrival at the campus she changes her mind when she sees other students with their parents unloading estate-car-loads of bags, boxes, instrument cases, portable TVs and stereo systems, kettles, racquets and even, in one case, skis.

"I know we're near the Pennines but I didn't think winter conditions were going to be that bad," Tamsin says, trying to sound flippant to cover up the awful feeling that she would rather go straight back home. She steps back hastily as a stack of cardboard boxes wobbles past above a pair of legs in black jeans. A saucepan sways precariously on top of the pile, its handle swinging gently like a drunken scanner.

"Saucepans! We didn't think of saucepans," Abigail says anxiously, lugging Tamsin's holdall.

"I'm sure I won't need kitchen stuff," Tamsin

says, "not in a hall of residence. Anyway, it saves washing up if you don't have anything to cook with."

"This time next year," Abigail says, "you'll be coming back to all the friends you haven't seen over the summer."

Tamsin tries to imagine herself as a seasoned second-year undergraduate. All the students arriving today are quite clearly newcomers who don't know each other yet; there is an air of enforced jollity as families part in the car park. Some of the arrivals look as conspicuously new and nervous as Tamsin feels. The campus is bewilderingly large, a new town built mainly in the ugly architectural style of the sixties, with signposts pointing to the Main Library, the Art Faculty, the Student Union, the Halls of Residence. Tamsin is to live in Edward Tarrant Hall. "E.T., everyone calls it," says one of the cheerful students on hand to greet newcomers. "The other one's J.P. – Joseph Preston."

E.T. and J.P. are adjacent brick buildings, three storeys high, on the edge of the campus, with grass areas and shrubs dividing them from the main lecture and administration areas. The helpful student shows Tamsin where to sign in and collect her keys, and leads the way inside. There is a tiled entrance lobby with pigeon-holes for mail, a reception desk and noticeboard, and a staircase leading up to a large common room. Tamsin's room is on the top floor, in a corridor of eight rooms, with a kitchen and bathroom handy and a laundry on the corridor opposite.

"Oh, this is lovely," Abigail says, as Tamsin opens the door to reveal a cube-shaped room with a bed, desk and a large window looking towards purplish moorland beyond the edges of the city. Tamsin goes straight to the window and looks out, pleased with the view.

"You've got everything you need here," Abigail says. "Washbasin, desk, shelves, reading light – you can soon put up some posters and make it look more lived-in."

"Yes, it's fine," Tamsin says, trying to banish the thought that the square room looks rather like a cell, and a wave of regret for her comfortable attic. This is her territory for the next year. This will be home.

None of the other rooms on the corridor seems to be occupied as yet, although music wafts up from an open window below. Abigail continues to look around the room, exclaiming at how comfortable it all is. Tamsin wishes she didn't have to *worry* so much about her mother. Driving all that way home on the motorway with no one to read the map. Going to Heathrow the day after tomorrow, to fly out to Claudia in Berlin. Then coming back home to the empty house. That's what Tamsin least likes to think about. Abigail has never lived on her own, apart from a few months in an awful bedsit before Tamsin was born (no wonder she's so impressed now, Tamsin thinks; she's probably comparing the hall of residence to her dingy hovel) which she has sometimes referred to as the worst time of her life. She won't like being on her own; there will be no one practical to change the fuses or mend the guttering, and if she gets involved in her painting she won't bother to eat properly. Fortunately Nan's house is only ten minutes' walk away, so she won't be altogether without company, but then what will happen if Nan gets ill again?

Tamsin sighs. She and her mother have shaped their lives around each other; they are props holding each other up. They are both entering unknown territory, alone.

It feels so final, going back downstairs with her mother once everything has been unloaded and brought up, standing by the car to make their inadequate farewells.

"Well, look after yourself."

"Drive carefully. And don't forget to check your tyre pressure and washer bottle every couple of weeks." Tamsin has always done these things and is sure they won't enter her mother's head.

"I won't. Don't work too hard. I'll hear from you in a day or two, then?"

They hug each other, and then Tamsin stands in the car park watching for her mother's final wave as the red Golf disappears from view, feeling suddenly bereft and alone, like an abandoned child. She feels as if her mother is leaving her for ever, and her life is changing irrevocably. It is totally stupid, because everything so far is just as she imagined it: here she is, at her first-choice university, about to embark on what should be the most rewarding years of her life, and what does she want to do at this precise moment? Go home with Mummy.

What if some new man has taken up residence by the time she goes home at Christmas? It won't even seem like home any more.

She tells herself not to be selfish about it. Mum is entitled to her own life. Tamsin's days of living at home are over; when she finishes her degree she will very probably want to work abroad. She has no right to interfere. If her mother meets someone she will have to be happy about it.

As usual, she is seeing only the worst possibilities. She gives herself a mental shake. Perhaps her mother will meet someone marvellous, who will suit her ideally, and there will be no need for regret or pretence. "You're a great one for crossing bridges before you get to them," her mother says, "and not only crossing, but *building* them." Tamsin acknowledges this to be true; she is cautious by nature. Perhaps she will grow out of it.

By next morning her nostalgia for home has subsided beneath the excitement of learning her way around and meeting innumerable people. There are queues to register for this and that, timetables to be collected, the maze of the campus to be negotiated, and various meetings: hall meetings, Faculty meetings, meetings with tutors. Tamsin thinks Friday is an odd day to start, but this has been arranged so that a weekend of Freshers' activities can follow before lectures start on Monday. Students other than first years won't be back until Sunday, apart from those organising the Freshers' Fair or the various discos, parties and pub crawls which are going on all weekend.

Tamsin's opposite neighbour in hall is called Josie and is doing Theatre Studies. She has a round face and wide round eyes, which add to her air of being amazed with everything. "Have you seen how big the Sports Centre is? Have you really got to go to all those lectures? We haven't got half as many. Have you seen that gorgeous-looking guy in the Admin Office? Are you really going to do Engineering? Why on earth do you want to do that?"

Josie makes friends easily, for which Tamsin is grateful. From the first evening on, she has only to sit down at a refectory table with Josie for three or four other people to wave and come over to join them. Finding out who your real friends are will take time, Tamsin suspects, but meanwhile it is nice to be part of a sociable group, even though most of Josie's acquaintances are doing arts subjects and think Tamsin is a bit peculiar to be studying Engineering.

"There are quite a few females doing Engineering," she defends herself, although looking around the refectory she can't actually see one. "There's nothing unusual about it." She has met the other students only briefly at a Faculty meeting, a wine-and-nibbles occasion where people said *Where do you come from?* and *What made you choose Engineering?* and stood about with glasses in their hands looking awkward or at ease according to temperament. There was an attractive Asian girl among three or four other females, but as Becky predicted the group was male-dominated.

"Are you vegetarian?" asks someone called Griselda, looking at Tamsin's plate of food. "I bet there aren't many vegetarian scientists."

"Why not?" Tamsin asks.

Griselda shrugs, as if it's obvious. "Well, why are you a vegetarian?"

"Because I don't like eating animals." Tamsin is always astonished by people's prejudices; she is sure that half the population views all scientists as bespectacled boffins doing unspeakable things to baby monkeys. Griselda looks rebuffed, and turns to say something in an undertone to the girl on her other side. Tamsin, who didn't mean to sound so abrupt, asks Griselda what subject she is taking, but the focus of attention has shifted. Josie and Tibor, a fellow drama student notable for his Slavic cheekbones, are doing a spoof of the ice-breaking activity their tutor made them do at their first group meeting. Perhaps being extrovert is a necessary quality for Theatre Studies. Tamsin envies people who feel socially at ease, like Josie, or some of the engineering students who talked airily about themselves to a group of strangers. Tamsin shrivels up in such situations. She envies Josie her magnet-like quality of drawing people to her and amusing them, without actually saying anything tremendously interesting or witty. Tamsin can't make out how she does it, but whenever Josie speaks everyone listens, as if she's about to utter something that mustn't be missed, or offer a definitive opinion.

"Is everyone going to the Freshers' Fair, then?" Tibor says, when he and Josie have finished their act.

"Yes, come on." Josie starts piling dishes on to a tray. "I don't want to miss the pub crawl afterwards."

The Freshers' Fair is in one of the main halls and consists of stands advertising dozens of clubs and societies, from the Real Ale Society to Christian Union, all vigorously touting for business. The atmosphere is festive, and for the first time Tamsin begins to feel that she is really here, part of it, not just an onlooker; there are all sorts of opportunities, social and otherwise. Detaching herself from the others, she gives a wide berth to Tiddlywinks Club (were they serious?) and Young Conservatives (were *they*?), signs up for Environment Concern and Animal Rights, and then pauses by Boghoppers. Walking-boots, generously caked with dried mud, dangle from a rail, and there is a table completely covered with out-spread Ordnance Survey maps, the Outdoor Leisure sort which show hills and peaks in close brown contours and craggy outlines. The near-ness of wild country – the Peak District, the Yorkshire Dales and even the Lakes – is a feature which helped to determine Tamsin's choice of university. This is one of the clubs she definitely wants to join.

As the only prospective customer at present, she is greeted with enthusiasm by one of the two stallholders. "There's a special outing for new members next Sunday, to Dovedale. Want me to put your name down?" He has very blue eyes, a spiky haircut and a Lancashire accent.

"Walking, or hopping?" Tamsin says, glancing at the Boghoppers sign, which is a cartoon picture of squat figures hopping over the gaps between capital letters, one clinging by fingernails to the sheer face of a squared-off B.

"You can hop if you like, but most people walk. Apart from Jim, that is." He looks round at his companion, who is sorting through a box of maps. "Jim's been known to go in for long-distance hopping, after he lost one of his boots in a river while he was playing at pioneers and wading across."

"Don't take any notice of Scott," Jim says affably, with a glance at Tamsin. "He was the one who dropped the boot in, but I notice he hasn't mentioned that."

"Anyway, it's easy walking on Sunday," Scott says, "mostly by the river and on the Tissington trail. No savage torrents or perilous summits. In fact the only hazard will be the mountain-bikes and the Sunday drivers. Just a stroll."

"Scott's idea of a stroll, that is." Jim flourishes a clipboard. "Sign up, sign up: expert guides, delightful scenery, pub stop a definite possibility, as he'll be leading."

"What are you signing up for, Tam?" Josie says, appearing beside her. Tamsin doesn't like being called Tam, but she lets it pass. "Not mountaineering? Are you serious?"

Tamsin sees the gleam of interest in Scott's eye and wonders again how Josie does it. It seems that she only has to open her mouth for everyone within range to be charmed.

"Want to come?" Scott says, taking the clipboard from Jim. "It's not climbing, just an easy walk. Mountains come later, once we've found out who's keen."

"When you've shown us the ropes, I suppose?" Josie says.

It's hardly an original joke, but Josie looks pleased with herself and Scott laughs appreciatively. "Oh, witty with it. I could make an obvious follow-up about getting into your stride, but I'll forbear. Peak District next Sunday, then?"

"Ooh, yes, I love the Peak District. Are you going, Tam? Shall I put us both down?"

She writes their names in a childish rounded script. Scott takes the clipboard back and reads what she has written. "Great. Josie Franklin and Tamsin Fox. Let me guess – you've got rooms next to each other in hall, right?"

"How did you know?" Josie says, round-eyed.

"Alphabetical order. There's a good chance you'll be best friends for life now, just because you happen to come next to each other in the alphabet."

"Yes, it's funny, isn't it?" Josie agrees. "My best friend at school was called Trudie Forrest."

Tamsin doesn't share this view at all, but it is pointless saying so as Scott is obviously talking only to Josie, her own presence all but forgotten. Real friendships can't be based solely on chance. Some people have already formed inseparable pairs or threesomes, but this is surely for the comfort of not being alone, rather than from real compatibility. Tamsin likes Josie but she does not think they will become best friends, and besides Josie is so gregarious that she doesn't need one close friend. There are hundreds of people on campus and it seems ridiculous to limit yourself to the first you happen to meet.

Tamsin notices that Jim is watching Scott with an amused half-smile, as if he has seen the chatting-up routine many times before. She has the vague sense that she knows Jim from some-where, but is unable to place him. He is taller and slimmer than Scott, with straight dark hair which flops over his forehead, and unremarkable features, but something in his expression chimes in her memory, making her wonder where she has seen him before. While she is thinking this he looks towards her and smiles, unsurprised to find her studying him. It's as if he already knows her too.

"Come on, Tam," Josie says. "I said I'd meet the others for the pub crawl. Are you coming?"

"See you on Sunday then, girls. Nine o'clock by the Union building," Scott says, handing the clipboard back to Jim, who reads the names and then glances at Tamsin again.

"He's nice, isn't he?" Josie says, meaning Scott, as they walk away.

"All right. Actually, I thought he was a bit patronising."

Josie's eyes open wide. "How do you mean?"

"You know – *see you then, girls*. Making us sound like a sort of commodity. We wouldn't have said *Cheerio then, boys*, would we?"

"He was only being friendly," Josie protests. "Are you a rampant feminist or something?"

"No, not rampant," Tamsin says, resisting another label. "Feminist, yes, I suppose so. Isn't everyone?"

Of the twenty new engineering students, only four are female. After the first seminar, Tamsin walks downstairs with Mike, one of the tutors (she can't get used to calling them by their first names; school habits are hard to break), who tells her, "In my experience, women who take engineering nearly always do well. They have to be determined or they wouldn't have got this far, whereas guys often drift into it. There's quite a high drop-out rate during the first year but I've never known a female student give up."

Tamsin isn't sure that everyone in the group rates female students so highly. When Mike asked them to get into threes for a problem-solving activity, some of them simply glanced at her and the other three girls as if they didn't count before moving into all-male huddles. Fortunately not everyone was like that. Tamsin teamed up with Ken, a friendly Glaswegian, and the Asian girl called Rikayah.

"Why might people drop out?" she asks Mike.

"A variety of reasons," Mike says. "They find out it's not for them, or they fail the first-year exams. After that, people tend to stick with it."

"Do many people fail?" Tamsin asks, not sure how reassured she is by women never dropping out; she doesn't want to be the exception.

Mike smiles. "Don't worry. You'll be all right."

Tamsin wonders how he can possibly claim to know after just one session. She joins the others for coffee in the refectory, where Toby, one of the more pushy members of the group, is explaining loudly why he chose to come here rather than to Oxford or Cambridge.

"Oxbridge would have been the obvious choice, of course," he informs everyone, "but that's why I didn't take it." He manages to give the impression that Admissions Tutors from both Oxford and Cambridge have been pleading for his favours. Tamsin collects her coffee and sits down next to Rikayah, and they exchange surreptitious smiles which mean *Isn't he a poser?* Although Rikayah is quiet, she doesn't miss much, Tamsin has decided.

After the break they head off for their first maths session. All the engineering students have to do maths, sharing lectures with those taking straight maths degrees. Tamsin has heard several people express doubts about it, expecting a high level of difficulty in a subject which is only of secondary interest to them. Tamsin enjoys maths because figures and concepts are reliable; they combine in predictable ways, they make patterns and relationshps with pleasing regularity, they do what's expected of them. Unlike people.

DOVEDALE

Dear Nan,

Here I am, a student, it's official! As I promised, you're getting my first letter. I hope you're still feeling better and not forgetting to take all those pills. I've put the phone numbers here at the top in case you ever need to ring while Mum isn't there, although there are only four phones for the whole hall of residence so it's not very easy to get through, but you could always leave a message.

Having been here a whole week now, I can drop the name of Fresher, which sounds like shower gel. I feel entitled to call myself Undergraduate now – far more dignified. The introductory fun and games are over and we've really started.

I expect Mum told you, I'm living in unashamed luxury here. I've got my own Room with a View (towards the moors) and everything I need, including nice neighbours with whom to share brews of coffee or sometimes even hot chocolate and biscuits at bedtime. If this sounds like midnight feasts in the dormitory, that's because it is! Lots of giggling and general silliness.

We have lectures every morning and practical sessions in the lab every afternoon. We've started on electronics this week, doing circuit diagrams. I suppose you must have done that sort of thing in the WAAF. There's a lot of maths, some of it quite difficult, but I'm managing all right so far (touch wood). The other students in my corridor are doing Theatre Studies, Geography, Modern Languages and Philosophy (that's two second-years). Those two like to sound highly intellectual, and wander along the corridor talking loudly about Heidegger and Existentialism and Socrates, carrying very weighty books (some of which look definitely unread). Meanwhile, no one can understand (or wants to) the problems I have trying to calculate output impedance. I'm beginning to feel a bit of an oddity in that respect. There's only one other first-year engineering student in the same hall, called Tatsuya. He's Japanese and lives on the ground floor (they keep us segregated to that extent, presumably so that you don't meet half-naked members of the opposite sex wandering in and out of the bathroom in the early hours) which will be handy if I get stuck with my work, especially as he's absolutely brilliant.

There are lots of clubs and societies on every subject you could think of and several you probably couldn't. So far I've limited myself to Environment Concern and Animal Rights (well, I couldn't pass *those by) and Boghoppers, which is the jolly name for the hill-walking group. I shall have to get a lot fitter before I embark on any mountain summits (don't worry, it's only the Peaks and Lake District, nursery slopes, not Everest the Hard Way). I don't suppose I shall be attempting anything too ambitious, considering I get dizzy going up a stepladder. We're off to the Peak District on Sunday for a walk in Dovedale – a chance to christen my new boots with some real moorland soil – so I'll tell you about it when I write next week.*

Look after yourself, and talking of stepladders don't do anything daft like trying to decorate the upstairs landing, which Mum said you were threatening to do – I can help you with it in the holidays.

Love, Tamsin.

Since the summer, Tamsin can't think about her grandmother without feeling that life is a weak, fragile thing. Nan's illness frightened Tamsin more than she wants to acknowledge. Nan was perfectly all right one day, taken into hospital with severe stomach pains the next.

Tamsin went straight from the Physics A-level exam to visit Nan in hospital. Outside the cool silence of the exam hall, the afternoon was so fiercely hot that the heat seemed to press down on the pavement with a physical force. It was Tamsin's last exam and she knew she had done well, but could not enjoy the feeling of relief that it was over or even wait around to discuss the paper with the other candidates. The whole summer was ahead of her now with no obligations apart from earning some money and waiting for the results, but Nan's sudden illness was a black hole threatening to suck Nan in, and Tamsin after her. Standing at the bus-stop with some younger pupils, Tamsin could hardly take in that her exams were finished, her life as a schoolgirl over, or that she was newly eighteen and an adult; she felt as helpless as a small child in the face of Nan's vulnerability to ageing and illness. Nan at my age had to be a lot tougher, she told herself. Nan had worked on a wartime bomber airfield, watching young men go off to get themselves killed. During her first few days on duty Nan had seen an aircraft crash in flames right in front of her, with the loss of its crew of seven; she had spoken to the pilot on the radio telephone just seconds before. And, Tamsin knows, this was a common enough experience in wartime – sad, but not unexpected. You just had to carry on with your job; you had no choice. You wouldn't have been much use to anyone if you were in tears all the time. It made Tamsin feel inadequate, imagining herself as Nan, wondering whether she could have coped, and doubting it. What use was passing exams if you collapsed in times of crisis?

The hospital alarmed her with its white-walled maze of echoing corridors and its air of efficient impersonality. She followed the signs to Nan's ward, passing Casualty and Ultrasound, Opthalmics and Pathology, trolleys parked in a bay, a hollow-eyed man in a plaid dressing-gown sitting outside Physiotherapy in a wheelchair. In the ward, the patients seemed lifeless and drained, like driftwood washed up on a beach, their limbs loose and heavy. The windows were open, the curtains swaying and lifting to the slight breeze, more animated than the pallid forms in bed. Neat, tight-waisted nurses moved about busily like worker ants, their brisk steps in shiny black shoes emphasising the gulf between action and passivity, energy and inertia. Tamsin paused at the ward entrance in dismay. Nan didn't belong here. She looked at the slack faces against white pillows; Nan couldn't be in here and still be Nan. The sleeping face of the elderly woman nearest her was grey, loose-skinned and vacant, as if character and life had already drained out of it. Tamsin's head whirled in panic. Beneath the clean and orderly surface of the hospital there were things that could not be controlled or cured. What if Nan were beyond help? What if she had some awful insidious disease, too late for treatment? What if Nan were destined to fade and weaken, with the nurses able to do no more than tidy her up and relieve her suffering?

Grandad's death from a heart attack three years ago shocked and bewildered Tamsin with its suddenness and finality. She could remember the helpless ache of grief, surrendering herself to it, wanting someone to come and soothe her and bring Grandad back, lovely Grandad Charlie. She could not bear it again . . .

And then she saw Nan, propping herself against the pillows, lifting a hand to wave.

"Visiting doesn't start till four." A young nurse stepped forward to intercept. "You're a bit early." And then, glancing up at the clock, "Oh well, it's only a few minutes. Go on then." She was not much older than Tamsin, with a pleasant smile that countered her air of starched officiousness.

Tamsin hurried towards Nan and bent to kiss her. Nan looked quite normal: a little tired, perhaps, but her hair was neatly brushed and her hazel eyes lively.

"Hello, love. How was your exam?" she asked, as if it were a perfectly ordinary afternoon and Tamsin had called in for a cup of tea on her way home from school.

Tamsin has discovered the swimming pool. From seven in the morning, and last thing at night, there is lane swimming, for early risers and the serious sporty types who carve their paths up and down with impressive fluidity and speed. Tamsin is not at all sporty, having been put off organised games at an early age because of having to wear glasses which got knocked off or spattered with mud, but swimming is the one thing she is quite good at. Most mornings she is there at seven, turning in the laps in her fast and effective breast-stroke, squinting short-sightedly because she can't wear her contact lenses for swimming. She wants to be fit enough for serious hill-walking once they get past the Sunday-stroll phase, but the swimming is enjoyable for its own sake, too. She likes the shock of the water, the sureness of her racing dive and thrust into cool blue, the surge and pull of her stroke. The exercise leaves her loose-limbed and relaxed, ready for the day, smelling slightly of chlorine which the changing-room showers cannot quite overcome.

"God, you're disgustingly healthy," Josie says, yawning and bleary-eyed in slippers and night-shirt, on her way to the loo as Tamsin comes back with wet hair and damp rolled towel. "What time is it?"

"Quarter to eight. Are you coming to break-fast?"

"Don't wind me up. It's the middle of the night."

Every morning Tamsin feels obliged to creep silently along the corridor to avoid waking the sleeping inhabitants. The outside world may be up and busy, but E.T. Hall sleeps until the last possible moment before the refectory stops serving breakfast at eight-thirty. Josie has never yet made it to breakfast since her one appearance on the first morning, and is often still asleep when the cleaner comes round at half-past nine. Tamsin always has nine o'clock lectures, whereas Josie's course involves fewer lectures with more back-ground reading, her official day not usually starting until ten. The corridor is seldom quiet before midnight, with people in and out of each other's rooms, doors slamming and music playing. Unable to adapt to the late-to-bed, late-to-rise routine, Tamsin is trying to develop her tolerance for loud laughter and thumping music while she is in the early stages of sleep. An ability like Josie's to sleep through anything would be a definite asset.

Early on Sunday, Tamsin's spirits rise as she looks out of her window in expectation of a good day. It is a golden October morning, the silver birches behind the hall throwing long shadows across dew-wet grass. She dresses quickly in jeans and a thick sweater and crosses the corridor to thump loudly on Josie's door, pausing for long enough to hear muffled grumbles from within. Josie will need breakfast if she's going to walk thirteen miles or so.

By nine o'clock they are on the coach outside the Student Union building. Jim is engrossed in a spread map showing the driver where to go, while Scott checks names from his clipboard and collects everyone's three pounds coach fare. He knows Josie's name without being prompted, but needs reminding of Tamsin's. The coach is not quite full, and once they are on their way out of the city towards the ring road he moves to the spare seat in front of Josie, turning round to talk to her. Tamsin, quite happy to leave them to it, gazes out

47

of the window at distant moorland rising to meet crisp blue sky. The motorway has cut an imperious groove through farms and grazing land, six lanes hard-shouldering aside the older, less aggressive lines of hedge, lane, byway: a new map overlaying the old. A good way south, the motorway is left behind and the land reasserts itself; the driver slows for narrow lanes where branches whip the coach roof, and for arched stone bridges where streams catch the light between steep banks.

The coach pulls up at a picnic site car park and everyone piles out, pulling on thick socks and boots and waterproof coats; the wind is cold enough for extra layers. Tamsin feels rather conscious of her almost-new walking boots, a birthday present from Nan, still shiny and unmarked and lovingly treated with Nikwax. The people who look like tough experienced walkers have boots very much worn and scuffed, especially around the toes. Josie is wearing Doc Martens with leggings randomly striped in black, green and purple, displaying long and very shapely legs like those of some exotic wading bird. Her lunch is in a stylish but totally impractical rucksack in tapestry dotted with mirror-work. Sensible outdoor clothing isn't Josie's style at all.

Scott heads off along a track leading into a meadow and along the bank of a stony river. Soon the party is strung out like bright beads on an uneven necklace: scarlet, kingfisher, royal blue.

Boots tramp rhythmically, swishing the long grass. The river is a band of light, fringed with purplish shadows where the alders crouch low. Here and there the surface is broken by a rock, making little glassy rushes and rapids. Tamsin stops to watch the quick flit and dash of a dipper, like a big tubby wren; she sees the flash of its white bib and then it stands motionless on a rock while the current swirls past, so that Tamsin wonders how it can keep its footing. She turns to point out the bird to Josie, but Josie isn't there. Instead, a little behind her, Jim stands looking out across the river.

"Yes, a dipper," he says. "You usually see one or two along here."

They watch until the bird darts into the water, reappears farther upstream, and then flies off. Jim falls into step beside Tamsin. As when she first saw him, she has an unaccountable sense of familiarity, as if she has known Jim for a long time and has walked with him like this before. She steals sidelong glances at him. He wears black jeans and a grey cable sweater, no coat, and carries a small rucksack. He walks with an easy, loping stride, effortlessly ground-covering, as if he would quickly outpace the rest of the group if he went at his own speed. Scott, walking ahead with Josie and telling her something that makes her laugh, is far stockier, with sturdy legs in bunchy socks and the sort of build Tamsin associates with foot-ballers. She wonders which kind of physique is best suited to long distances and mountain walking, and then why she feels no need to make conversation with Jim, even though she is curious about him. She is glad that he doesn't make small talk of the *How are you settling in?* and *Where do you come from?* variety. His eyes are narrowed against the glint of sunlight on water as he gazes ahead to the bend in the river. He looks quite at ease, as if he has expected the day to be pleasurable and is not disappointed. Tamsin wonders whether he shares her sense that they have met before, but it would sound too corny to ask.

He waits for her to go in front through a squeeze-stile and then remarks, "Tamsin's an unusual name."

She is surprised that he remembers.

"It's a variation of Thomas,' she explains, "or Thomasina."

"Yes, I know," he says. "Like Thomasin Yeobright in *The Return of the Native*."

"Thomas Hardy? I haven't read that one, but I did *Far from the Madding Crowd* for GCSE. I know you shouldn't say you've *done* something, as if you've finished with it or got it out of the way. My English teacher used to go berserk if anyone said that."

"Thomas Hardy can stand more than one doing," Jim says. "You should try *Return of the Native*. You'd like it."

"How do you know?"

"I don't, but I bet you would. Read it and tell me."

"I'm not sure how much time I'm going to have for proper reading," Tamsin says apologetically, since Jim is evidently a reader. "I mean novels and things. I'm always writing up my lecture notes."

Jim nods. "Reading's what I'm supposed to spend my time doing. My flatmates think my course is a holiday compared to theirs. What they call work is peering down a microscope or studying rock formations. I can never convince them that lounging about with a book is anything like work."

"You're doing English?"

"Yes. Final year," Jim says. "And you're that still quite rare thing, a female engineer."

Tamsin stares at him. "I am, or will be, but how did you know?"

"Aha," Jim says. "We have our sources. Scott makes it his business to investigate all new female students, as you've probably noticed. Your friend came round to our flat for coffee the other night and she mentioned you."

"Josie?" Tamsin doesn't know why she should feel so surprised. Josie didn't say anything about going round to Scott's and Jim's flat, wherever it is; not that there's any reason why she should account for her movements. It wouldn't surprise Tamsin to learn that Josie knows everyone on the campus by now.

"The one with the striped legs and witty banter, yes," Jim says. "She and Scott had been playing squash."

Tamsin has the impression that he and Scott, though friends, are not much alike.

"What attracts you to engineering?" Jim asks, and because he seems genuinely interested, rather than making the trite what-an-odd-choice-for-a-girl sort of enquiry she has become used to, she is about to reply in detail. But a shout from ahead forestalls her.

"Oi, Jim! Come up here! You've got a better map."

The group at the front has come to a halt by a choice of stiles. Jim strides on to catch up, looking round at Tamsin as if he expects her to follow and continue the conversation, but she stays at the back of the group. The route-finding problem resolved, they make their way up a tussocky hillside, watched by wary sheep. Tamsin falls into conversation with a girl called Fiona who tells her about a recent youth-hostelling trip to Scotland.

"We go on quite a few weekend trips each year," Fiona says when Tamsin expresses interest, "to Wales or the Lakes. The next one's probably full up, but ask Jim about it if you like. He's organising it."

"Thanks," Tamsin says. But although she would like to go to Wales or the Lake District, she has no intention of approaching Jim on the subject.

THE WEARING OF THE GREEN

On Wednesday evening Tamsin and Rikayah go to a joint meeting of the Animal Rights and Environment Concern groups. The girl called Harry who organises the Animal Rights group is eager to get the two groups combined against the proposed Criminal Justice Bill. She addresses her audience with the same determination Tamsin has already seen her apply to the campaign against the export of live food animals.

"Have you thought what it means if this goes through?" she demands, as if accusing everyone of complacency. "You have a civil right, or at least you *did* have, to protest about anything you choose. This bunch of Fascists, the government, want to take that away. The police will be able to stop us from doing anti-hunt protests, which we've always done – they'll be able to turn us back on the roads and footpaths and stop us from going anywhere *near* a hunt."

"That's right," agrees someone with a Birmingham accent. "The police often say they're on our side against hunting but they've got to make sure it can take place even so. With this new law we'll be powerless. They'll even be able to turn us off public rights of way."

"They want to make us into criminals!" Harry continues. "Wait till you want to protest about a road-building scheme that happens to mean the digging up of ancient woodland. Stand in front of a JCB and you'll be committing a criminal act. You could leave college with a criminal record, just for trying to put your point across to a government who won't listen! Do you realise what that will mean when you try to get a job? It's moral blackmail! They want to frighten everyone into keeping quiet, so they can build their motorways and carry on killing animals for fun. And this is supposed to be a democracy!"

There are murmurs of agreement, and someone asks, "So what do you want us to do about it, Harry?"

What Harry wants them to do is to write to their MPs at home, petition everyone on campus, and campaign in the main shopping area with petitions and leaflets. Accordingly, Tamsin and Rikayah, equipped with KILL THE BILL badges and literature, enter the brand-new shopping mall on Saturday for the first time. It is pristine, anonymous, an enclosed conservatory-like space with a roof of glass panes held in suspension by a web of green girders, the ground level echoing to the clop of feet past raised brick shrubberies, garden-style benches, a central fountain. Wide entrances entice shoppers into The Gap, River Island, The Body Shop. Tamsin has the odd feeling of forgetting where she is; the mall could have been plonked down anywhere in Britain. Hardly have she and Rikayah established themselves by the water feature when a uniformed security officer tells them that they can't petition here without advance permission from the management, which they haven't got. They will have to go outside in the rain.

In the grey October drizzle the city presents a different face. Buses swish past, spraying pedestrians with grimy water. There are real smells out here, fumes and dampened dirt, and ground coffee from a delicatessen. The street here is more traditional: a second-hand bookshop, a window display of musical instruments, a gentleman's outfitters. Tamsin can't help seeing it as a black-and-white photograph, Edwardian, with trams and blinds, shopkeepers in ankle-length aprons, windows festooned with sausage strings and game birds. The new and the old rub shoulders like different generations in a photograph album. Tamsin and Rikayah look around for the most suitable spot, decide on the colonnaded entrance to the public library and prepare to get wet.

Unfortunately the issue takes quite a lot of

explaining, and they receive suspicious looks from some people who either think they are asking for money or take them for organisers of illegal student raves.

"Next time I'm going to petition for SAVE THE WHALE," Rikayah says. "Something people don't need convincing about."

Tamsin lifts a corner of her soggy sheaf of papers. "I did better on campus – I'd already filled in five sheets. Let's stop next time one of us gets to the bottom of a page, and go somewhere for a cup of tea."

They eye passers-by hopefully until at last Rikayah's page is filled. She gives Tamsin a thumbs-up signal and they abandon their post with relief. Finding a tea-shop with tempting displays of patisserie in the window, they go into the Earl Grey warmth, draping their wet coats over chair-backs.

"I think we've earned a bit of decadence," Rikayah says.

Tamsin picks up the menu. "Talking of decadence, did you hear what that man said to me, the one with the miserable-looking dog? He said, 'The police need more powers if you ask me. Ought to be allowed to lock up all you student troublemakers, living off taxpayers' money to pay for your drugs and booze.' We've turned into stereotypes."

"Well, just look at us. You can see we mean trouble."

They giggle at the idea of being labelled as rabble-rousers, since no one could look less offensive than they do at present, ordering tea in the demure Laura Ashley café.

"No wonder his dog looked fed up," Rikayah says. "Living off the taxpayer, am I? Does that mean I don't have to repay my student loan?"

Dear Mum, Tamsin writes,

Thanks for the postcard. Here's one of Dovedale, where I went walking last Sunday. Glad you had a good time in Berlin with Claudia. How was your German, and did you bring back a piece of the Wall?

I'm working hard but enjoying it, and finding time to do other things as well – hence the card.

You haven't mentioned the Lonely Hearts! Were they piled up on the doorstep when you got back?

Love, T.

Tamsin rather hopes not; she has already had enough of Romance at second hand. Julia, one of the second-year students on Tamsin's corridor, is heavily involved with some man Tamsin has not yet seen. The relationship seems to be as full of incident as a TV soap, since Julia's mood veers wildly between extremes which affect the atmosphere of the whole corridor. On bad days she droops about, red-eyed and dressing-gowned, receiving comfort and herbal tea from her friends and refusing to go down for meals, emerging only to whisper anguished phrases into the telephone. Equally unpredictably, she rushes from room to room in wild excitement seeking advice on various combinations of clothes and make-up before teetering off in high heels and a cloud of perfume, a style which surely no one would adopt for a fellow student. Whoever this man is, he seems to keep her in a state of perpetual agitation. Tamsin hopes he's worth it. If this is what Love can do to you, she will manage without, thanks.

She has taken to working in the library after supper on most evenings, sometimes alone, sometimes with Rikayah or Tatsuya, until closing time at nine. It is easier to work here than in hall, without the distractions of laughter, music, boiling kettles and whirring hairdriers, or Julia's latest drama. When she comes back, her work finished, she can abandon herself to chatter and coffee-brewing.

The main library is warm and spacious. Tamsin has chosen a regular spot for herself, at the back near the art section, where the table is large enough to spread out her books and lecture notes. There is a soft humming from the fluorescent light tubes, occasional footsteps in the gallery overhead, a discreet cough from an adjoining bay, sounds which rise and fall like soft waves at the edge of her thought processes. She is engrossed in her amplification calculations, working quickly in pencil, following the examples they have worked through in groups. Conscious of someone approaching and sitting in the chair opposite, she does not look up until she has written down the next stage of the equation. She expects it to be Rikayah or Tatsuya, but instead it's Jim, leafing through a book on Edvard Munch and apparently waiting for her to notice him.

She is surprised only by her lack of surprise. She has not seen Jim since the Dovedale outing but for some reason she knew he would turn up again before long.

He looks across at her equation. "What on earth does that mean, all those Zs? Or are you dozing off?"

"It can have that effect," Tamsin says. "Well, the Zs mean different things. Zi and Zo. Zi is input impedance and Zo is output impedance."

"Greek to me," Jim says. He looks back over his shoulder at the clock above the issue desk. "Ten minutes to closing. What about a drink when you're finally chucked out of here? Or will Zi and Zo take up your entire Friday night?"

"All right. Thanks," she says, since she can't really think of any reason why not. It is Friday after all, and Josie will probably be in the bar with Tibor and the others, or maybe with Scott.

"See you outside then," Jim says. "I've left my books upstairs."

When she packs up and leaves he is waiting for her outside the security gates, tall, angular, with his books bulging out of the green rucksack he carried on the walk, which is slung over one shoulder. Apart from the books, he looks as if he is about to set off on a hike: he is wearing a green Gore-Tex coat, the same grey cable sweater, black jeans and laced boots. Collecting her own coat from the rail, Tamsin is suddenly doubtful. If Josie and the others see her come into the bar with Jim, they will try to make something of it. She tells herself that walking from the library to the bar with someone is hardly incriminating; she should take things more casually, like everyone else. However, when they get outside Jim turns right towards the porter's lodge instead of left towards the Union building and bar, and Tamsin stops in confusion.

"I thought you meant the Union bar?"

"Oh." Jim looks down, scuffing the heel of one boot on the gravel path. "Well, we could go there, but I was thinking of Rafferty's, the Irish pub in town. Have you been there yet?"

"No."

"Would you like to give it a try? They have live music on Friday nights."

"OK. Sounds nice."

They leave their bags at the porter's lodge. The night is damp, mild, smelling of earth and leaves, the pavements shining in pools of light under street lamps. Tamsin is reminded that the city has a life separate from the university: normal life, Friday-night life, with people wandering about eating chips or hamburgers or drifting towards the pubs and cinemas. The Irish pub is a dark fug of Guinness-smelling warmth and lively conversation, with someone playing the fiddle. Jim steers Tamsin towards a small corner table and makes his way through the crush at the bar. She waits for him, listening to Irish accents nearby and looking at the pub décor, all mahogany browns and rich greens. On the wall opposite is a photograph of the Irish football team, with a tricoloured scarf draped over the frame. The pub is pretending to be in Dublin, with street signs displayed around the walls, names Tamsin knows: O'Connell Street, Grafton Street, St Stephen's Green. She is not quite sure how she got herself into this situation or whether she wants to be in it; coming to a pub out of college with Jim is a bit different from going to the Union bar. She doesn't know why it seems inevitable that Jim should seem drawn to her, at least to the extent of wanting to get to know her better, just as she is drawn to him. His choice of an Irish pub is odd too, with its Dublin ambience and echoes of her family past.

She tells herself, no, it is not inevitable: I have a choice in the matter. I could have a quick drink and go, or I could get up and leave now, before he comes back from the bar.

But she doesn't, and Jim catches her eye and smiles as he weaves his way back with two brimming glasses. He sits down and says, "You still haven't told me why you chose Engineering."

He is drinking Guinness. Tamsin looks at the rich dark liquid with its creamy top settling like a duvet, and remembers her visit to the Guinness Brewery in Dublin with Mum and Nan and Grandad. Horses pulling the big drays, a carpentry shop where strips of wood are made into barrels, the rich malty smell of the brew filling the air. Grandad Charlie and Mum drank Guinness at the end of the tour, but Nan would only sip at it, wrinkling her nose. Tamsin drank orange juice, wondering how grown-ups could like something so tarry and horrible, worse than medicine. Perhaps she will tell Jim about it in a minute, her holiday in Ireland.

"Well," she answers, "I like knowing how things work. I like *making* things work. Principles, patterns, theories that work when you apply them, just as they should. And I want to do something useful, something that has an obvious practical application."

Jim is leaning forward to listen above the noise of fiddle music and gales of laughter, one hand clasping his glass. He nods slowly. "What do you want to specialise in?"

"Civil engineering, I think. I'd like to design waterways and irrigation schemes, perhaps in the Third World. But I don't have to specialise for another two years. What about you? What are you going to do after this year?"

"I don't know," Jim says. "Listening to you makes me feel a bit aimless. I've just drifted into an English degree because I didn't know what else to do. Afterwards I suppose I'll drift into whatever I can find. You seem to know exactly what you want."

"Yes, but only because work is the one area of my life where I feel in control." Tamsin is surprised to find herself saying something so personal to someone she hardly knows; she isn't much given to discussing her feelings. She says hastily, "Is it very hard work in your final year?"

Jim looks at her speculatively before answering. Then he says, "It ought to be. But I'm not really all that dedicated. I do what needs to be done and I'm probably safe for a lower second, maybe a two-one if the wind's behind me. There are one or two in my group who are going all out for firsts. You never see them – they're always having extra tutorials or slogging at their dissertations. That's all right for them, but I think university's for having fun as well. Doing the things you want to do."

Tamsin thinks of what Aunt Rachel said to her when she came to stay while Nan was in hospital: Make sure you have some fun as well, Tamsin. Don't work all the time. It's not just about getting a degree. You'll have chances at university you might never have again.

"That's exactly what my aunt told me," she says. "Although she did get a first, at Oxford. I think she worked hard *and* had fun."

"Do you come from an intellectual family, then?" Jim looks a bit daunted.

"No! My mum left school at sixteen and then packed in her secretarial course because she got bored with it. She couldn't get out of school fast enough. I don't mean that she's unintelligent," Tamsin says, "but certainly not academic."

"And your father?"

"I haven't got one." Tamsin usually leaves it at that, but now for honesty's sake she adds, "At least, I have got a father – somewhere – but I've never met him. My mum isn't married and they split up before I was born."

Jim looks interested, but before he can pursue it, if he is going to, she asks him, "What about you? Where does your family come from?"

"Kent, near Canterbury. That's partly why I'm here – we're fairly close to wild country and good climbing. East Kent's about as far from mountains as you can get."

"Same here. I've never done any mountain-walking, but I want to. What about you? Do you really prefer rock-climbing?"

"I like climbing, but I'm just as happy to go on a good walk. There are three or four of us who go climbing quite often – Dave, Scott and me usually. We go down to the Peaks for odd days and up to Scotland or North Wales a couple of times over the winter. But we don't do anything specially difficult, not what you'd call mountaineering." He looks at her and adds, "You should stay with the group if you want to go mountain-walking. There are some good weekend trips coming up."

Tamsin feels encouraged. She notices that Jim's glass is nearly empty, while her own half-pint of lager is standing on the table almost forgotten. She swallows some more, to keep up. A gravelly voice has joined the fiddle, and she notices that Jim is listening intently. Tamsin listens too, making out the words: *The shamrock is forbid by law to grow on Irish ground.* It's an Irish rebel song, one that has always reminded Tamsin of her great-grandfather and his involvement in the Dublin Rising of 1916. Her confusion about all-Ireland then, Northern Ireland now, Loyalists, Republicans, partition, has gradually fitted together and made sense, as much as a senseless situation can. The past makes a seamless join with the present, old injustices leading straight to the bombings and retaliations of recent years and the current uneasy truce.

"Are you Irish?" she asks Jim, "or specially interested in Ireland?"

"My father is," Jim says. "He came over from County Cork when he was a boy. And I've got an Irish name, McGrath."

Jim McGrath. James McGrath. She tries it out silently.

"You haven't got an Irish accent," she remarks.

"You should hear my old feller. He has a

voice would charm the hinges off the gates of hell," Jim says in broad Cork. "And were you ever in Ireland itself?"

"Yes." At that point voices around them swell into the chorus of the song, and Tamsin can't help joining in softly: *She's the most distressful country that ever yet was seen; They're hanging men and women there for the wearing of the green.*

Jim's expression snaps into alertness. He puts down his glass and stares at her. His eyes are very dark brown, like the Guinness. "You know that song?" he asks, surprised back into his normal voice.

"Yes. My grandfather used to sing it. He liked Irish songs."

"Is he Irish, then?"

"No, but my great-grandfather was. He was in Dublin during the Easter Rising. He got shot in O'Connell Street."

"You're kidding! Do you mean he was killed in the Rising?"

"No, he wasn't killed, not then. He was shot again though, and killed outright, a few years later in the civil war. He didn't really know which side he was on in the Rising. He wanted Ireland to be independent but he was an officer in the British army during the First World War. My grandmother says he was on both sides at once."

"Good God!" Jim sways back in his chair and clutches the arms. "I've been reading up about 1916 and all that, the last few days – I'm doing

Irish literature for my dissertation – and it turns out your great-grandad was there along with Pearse and Connolly . . . !" He looks at her with immense respect, as if she has come straight from the conflict of 1916, rubbing shoulders with the rebels.

Tamsin is beginning to feel peculiar, and she hasn't had enough lager to be drunk. To give herself time to collect her thoughts, she goes up to the bar to buy a round. She almost wishes she hadn't told Jim about her great-grandfather; he is so impressed that it feels like producing an unbeatable trump card. Waiting to be noticed – she always feels invisible at bar counters – she looks across at him. He is listening to the singer – *the wind that shook the barley* – with legs stretched out, elbows resting on the arms of the chair. There is an unravelling hole in one sleeve of his sweater. While they have been talking she hasn't been able to help noticing that he is really quite fanciable, though not in any obvious or self-regarding way. His dark hair is longish, growing just anyhow, not like Scott's which looks as if it's blow-dried every morning; he gives the impression of not caring much about his appearance, wearing whatever comfortable clothes come to hand. He is relaxed, waiting for her, with the air he has of being perfectly contented with whatever situation he finds himself in. Tamsin decides to stop worrying about what she says, or doesn't say, or what people might think: it doesn't matter. She has an inexplicable sense of finding someone she has known for a long time, someone she will find again.

When she sits down with the drinks, Jim says, "What happened to him, then, your great-grandfather?"

"He was killed by mistake," she says. "He was married to my great-grandmother by then, and they were living in Dublin. His name was Patrick Leary and he was an artist."

After Dublin, Nan had taken her and Mum and Grandad Charlie to the place where it happened. Tamsin can remember standing by the seashore at low tide, looking out across the broad sweep of bay, the river estuary an urban interruption of grey chimneys and cranes and warehouses. The wind lifted her hair, chill enough to raise the hairs on her arms into gooseflesh. Nan stood beside her, holding her hand, explaining. "He was a soldier, you see, in the war. The Great War, not my and Grandad's war. It was even longer ago. He went back to the war and that was where he met my mother, Alice – she was a nurse, in France. But he was always close to the big guns, because that was his job when he went back, and it made him a bit deaf."

They were all listening intently. The grown-ups knew the story, but they hadn't been here before. The sands were smooth, ivory paleness merging into ivory-blue at the sea's edge. A boy and a dog ran along the tideline, kicking up spray. It was not a place for death. Further along, there were boat-huts made of blackened wood, a few dinghies marooned on the sand, ropes, lobster-pots.

"He was a painter, like Mum," Nan continued, "and he loved to wander about by the sea, sketching, or just thinking. There were guns hidden down here in the boat-huts, boxes of them – there was fighting going on by then, you see –"

"Who was fighting?" Tamsin asked. "Were there Germans here?"

"Not *the* war," Nan said. "A different sort of war. Irish against Irish by that time. And some-one thought he was after the guns, and shouted out a warning to him, and he didn't hear so of course he took no notice. And they shot him."

It sounded to Tamsin like the sort of thing that happened on television. Men chasing each other, hiding behind cars, running up iron staircases and leaping across rooftops, aiming guns at each other. It was a man's game, shooting, being on different sides. But not a game here. The man who was going to be Nan's father had died, through a mistake. Mum listened as if to a story about a stranger, but Nan was sad, looking down to the beach as if she could see her lost father. Tamsin looked towards the boat-hut which cast a dark shadow on the sand, and imagined she could see him too, walking along the shoreline where the boy and the dog were running a few minutes ago. He was wrapped up in his thoughts, not hearing, not really even seeing, like Mum when she was thinking about a painting. And the person who shouted would have stood just here, Tamsin thought, with a gun aimed. The shot splitting the air, punctuating the silence like a full stop.

She hasn't spoken about it for a long time. Telling the story to Jim, she watches it happening in front of her like a silent film, with the slow inevitability of tragedy. It is part of her family's heritage of pride and sorrow; love is swiftly followed by loss in each generation in turn. Tamsin fears a trap, spring-loaded with the weight of the past, waiting for her to walk too close.

"Did you think, when you first saw me," she asks Jim, who has listened in silence while she talked, "that we'd seen each other somewhere before?"

He looks blank. "No. Should I have?"

KINDER PLATEAU

"Do you want to come on a youth-hostelling weekend at Edale?" Jim asks when they get back to campus. "Walking, not climbing. There's a few of us going, Friday night to Sunday. We're going to do Kinder Scout and the beginning of the Pennine Way on Saturday and then probably Mam Tor or some other shorter walk on the Sunday. Nothing difficult, just a bit boggy if it's wet, which it certainly will be, this time of year."

Tamsin is tempted. "Who else is going?"

"Scott, Glyn, Whistler –"

"Whistler? As in Whistler's Mother?"

"That's the one. He lives in our flat. He doesn't whistle, not excessively anyway. We call him Whistler because his name's James McNeill, and having two Jims in one flat would be confusing. He comes in useful because he's a mature student, i.e. twenty-five, and the only one old enough to drive the minibus. Then there's Fiona, Candida, Jane, Louise, Dave, I can't remember who else, but we've got a spare place because someone had to drop out."

"But I don't belong to the Youth Hostel Association."

"That's all right. It's a group booking. We haven't worked out the cost yet but it won't be much, just a fiver or so for the minibus and then the youth hostel fees."

"OK then, thanks. I'd like to."

"Great," Jim says, and they part outside E.T. Tamsin goes up to her room, wondering whether she should have asked him up for coffee. She bypasses sounds of drunken frivolity from Josie's room and then spends the next hour and a half sleeplessly worrying because she won't know anyone on the Edale weekend and might be so slow at climbing hills that she will hold up the entire group.

Rikayah's family – parents and little sisters – drive up from south London to stay for the weekend. Tamsin guesses that many students would rather die than have their parents staying on campus, but Rikayah's family is obviously a very close one. She has booked guest rooms for them and invites Tamsin over to meet them on Saturday afternoon.

In Rikayah's room in Joseph Preston, Tamsin is astonished by her friend's appearance. Usually Rikayah dresses in jeans and leggings and baggy jumpers like everyone else, but today she wears shalwar Kameez: a tunic of kingfisher blue with an embroidered front panel, satin trousers of deep glowing red, a long scarf in the same shade. Her feet are in sandals and she wears elaborate gold earrings which gleam against her skin. She and her family are like exotic humming-birds perched among the plain furnishings. Tamsin, in jumper and jeans, feels exceptionally drab. Rikayah's parents greet her warmly, and she enjoys being accepted into their circle. She has always wondered what it would be like to be part of a proper family.

Rikayah makes Yunaan tea for everyone and they eat delicious sweet cakes made by her mother. When Tamsin eventually gets up to go, there is a chorus of goodbyes as if she is an established family member, and Rikayah's father gets up to open the door for her and wish her a formal farewell. "We're pleased that Rikayah has made such a charming friend," he tells her.

In the lab on Monday, Tamsin asks Rikayah, "Do you often wear traditional dress? You look great in it."

"Always for family occasions," Rikayah answers. "My parents like to see me looking like a demure young daughter. We're a very traditional family in some ways. My grandparents are first generation immigrants – we're Kenyan Asians. They run a grocer's shop and my grandmother doesn't speak much English and always wears a sari. In fact, when you said the other day that we'd become student stereotypes, I felt pleased to be a different kind of stereotype. We've never lived in Asia but to many of the local people at home we must be Pakis, and our shop's known as the Paki shop."

Labels, Tamsin thinks. At least here there's no chance of anyone calling Rikayah a Paki. The multi-cultural mix of the campus is taken for granted.

The week passes very satisfactorily. Tamsin's group goes on a site visit to examine the construction of a motorway interchange; a visiting speaker lectures on engineering design. She completes her first project and presentation, a circuit design for a computer room, and gets a good mark for it, although in fairness she thinks two- thirds of the marks were due to her partner, Tatsuya, whose mental leaps she sometimes finds hard to follow. She starts to learn about computer-aided design and familiarises herself with electronic mail. She swims every morning, plays badminton with Rikayah and table-tennis with Tatsuya; she goes to the film club on Wednesday evening, drinks in the bar with Josie and Griselda and Tibor, and collects more signatures for her petition. She has a domestic session of washing and ironing and gossip with Josie; she drinks tea and coffee and cocoa increasingly late into the night and feels sleepy in the afternoons. She is learning to be a student.

* * *

Phoning home, she asks for an update on the Lonely Hearts.

"Well, yes, there are one or two who sound reasonable," Abigail says. "I've even met one of them. Twice."

"Oh? What was he like?"

"Nice enough to go out with again, at least."

"Mum, are you sure you –"

Abigail laughs. "Yes, I know. Don't go to strange places with strange men. You've gone over it all enough times. Make sure *you're* as careful. How are you getting on? Are you socialising much? I hope you're not working too hard."

Tamsin gives her an update, telling her mother about the visit and the project, Rikayah's family, the swimming, and the forthcoming weekend at Edale. She doesn't mention going to the pub with Jim.

A minibus is parked outside the Student Union building in good time on Friday after lectures, but there is no one in sight. Tamsin dumps her bag on the ground, hoping this is the right bus. Soon a chattering female group, some of whom Tamsin recognises from the Dovedale trip, emerges from the foyer, loaded with bags and rucksacks and boots which they proceed to stow inside the bus, stashing things in every corner and under the seats. One of them, a plump girl with curly brown hair, notices Tamsin and says, "Are you coming with us?"

"Yes," Tamsin says, feeling like a new girl at school. She will be sharing a dormitory with this confident group of friends.

"Better bag a place then. Here, pass me your stuff."

Tamsin gets in and sits at the back. More people arrive, including a lanky figure with short blond hair and a bony face, who gets in at the driver's door.

"Hi, Whistler. Got you on chauffeuring again, have they?" someone says.

"For my sins." Whistler settles into his seat and starts adjusting the mirror, tugging at the gear lever, flipping through the pages of the log book. He looks round to see who's on the bus. "Oh God, we haven't got to put up with Louise all weekend, have we?" He has a broad Glaswegian accent.

Louise is the friendly one who spoke to Tamsin. "That's your privilege," she says archly. "Do you know anyone here?" she asks Tamsin. "What's your name?" She points out Candida, Jane, Whistler – "don't take any notice of him, he's always like that" – Andy and Jon, who seem to be a pair; Dave, Helen, Glyn and Fiona, who Tamsin recognises.

"Scott will be here in a minute," Louise says. "He's late as usual. Was it Scott who got you to come?"

"No, it was Jim," Tamsin says.

Candida, who is sitting next to Fiona, turns and looks at her sharply.

"Where *is* Jim?" Glyn asks. "He hasn't dropped out, has he?"

"Don't be daft," Candida says. "It would take an earthquake to make Jim drop out. And anyway, he's made the booking."

"We won't get far without him," Whistler points out from the front. "He's got all the maps."

"What's the weather going to be like?"

"Wet."

"It's always wet at Edale. Have you got good waterproof gear?" Louise asks Tamsin.

"I've got some, but I don't know how much wet it can stand up to." Tamsin has bought herself a cheap kagoule and overtrousers, her finances not being up to the expense of Gore-Tex. Perhaps she will need to drop a few hints before Christmas.

Glyn, small and dark and Welsh, starts telling them how he got stuck in a bog on the Pennine Way: "There I am, up to my waist, can't move without falling face down in the stuff, when I see this army helicopter flying towards me. So I wave frantically and yell for all I'm worth, and what do they do? They wave back as if they think I'm enjoying myself, up to the armpits in sludge for the sheer fun of it, and they fly straight past . . ."

"Here's Jim," Fiona says, rubbing at the side window which is already steaming up, "and Scott."

There is a jeering chorus of "About time too"

and "Always last" as Jim leans in at the front to dump a wodge of maps on the front seat, and then comes round to the back with his gear. He smiles at Tamsin and passes in his rucksack and a pair of heavy, very large boots, which she stows in the diminishing space under her seat, while Scott clambers forward to sit next to Louise. Jim gets into the front passenger seat and opens up a road map.

It is already dusk as the minibus pulls out of the campus, full of chatter and laughter and shouted insults. They all seem to know each other very well. Everyone's weaknesses and foibles are exposed, joked about, exaggerated: Louise's missed course-work deadline, Candida's posh boyfriend, Whistler's recent mistake in turning up at the wrong hostel in Scotland, Jim's travelling library: "What have you got in your rucksack this time, then? It was the complete works of James Joyce last time. Or have you discovered any decent English writers yet?"

"You realise he never actually reads any of it," Whistler says. "It's all for show. Either that, or he thinks if he carries it about in his rucksack it'll filter into his brain by osmosis."

Jim doesn't say much, concentrating on his map-reading, occasionally retaliating when the teasing is directed at him. Tamsin feels a bit out of it, although Louise occasionally turns round to explain a running joke. Meanwhile, she observes the others. Scott, Louise and Whistler are the extroverts of the group; Glyn joins in intermitt-ently, and Candida, who is rather beautiful, is good at haughty put-downs. She has a mane of tawny hair which she seems very conscious of, frequently running her fingers through it or throwing it back so that it flies into Tamsin's face. Tamsin can't imagine her getting muddy or soaked and not minding.

The Friday-night traffic makes the journey a stop-and-start one until they are clear of the motorway, and they reach Edale only just in time for the evening meal. The Youth Hostel is set amid trees up a winding track bordered by sheep fences; at the top, several cars and mini-buses are parked near the outbuildings and in front of the pillared porch of the main house. Getting out, Tamsin smells the tang of conifers, and senses the moors rising behind the house in dark misty silence, unapproachable until day-light. The air is different here, cold and sharp, as clean as iced water. They check in at the warden's office in the entrance hall of the once-grand house. Their accommodation is in a self-contained outbuilding called The Edges, which comprises dormitories sleeping six or seven people. After the meal, the group splits into two. Some people want to go down to the pub nearly two miles away, and as Whistler doesn't want to drive again they are proposing to walk; the rest plan to stay and play cards. As Jim seems to be joining the pub group, Tamsin makes up her mind to stay behind; she doesn't want to appear to be tagging along with him, and has decided by now that he only asked her along to fill up the spare place, rather than from the personal interest she suspected at first. However, while she is looking at the noticeboard in the entrance hall waiting for Jon and Andy to bring the playing cards, Jim comes up to her and says, "Won't you come? It's not raining now. I wish you would."

Well, on second thoughts, she decides, a walk in the fresh air does sound like a good idea; and I'm not much good at card games anyway.

Later, curled up in her sheet sleeping-bag on a top bunk and half-dozing, Tamsin listens to Candida, Jane and Louise getting ready for bed. Their voices float into her semi-consciousness. They are discussing people she doesn't know, and then Jane remarks, "You didn't tell me Jim was bring-ing his new girlfriend along."

There is an edge of sarcasm to her voice, and for a moment Tamsin wonders sleepily who she can mean. A humph comes from the bunk under-neath, which is Candida's, followed by the sound of brisk rummaging in a bag.

"Tamsin?" Louise says. "Is he going out with her then?"

"Looks like it, doesn't it?" Jane says from the washbasin. "That's one in the eye for you, Cand."

"Doesn't matter to me," Candida retorts. "Why should it?"

Saturday is damp and misty, heavy clouds gathering. After breakfast the group sets off across squelchy fields to the official start of the Pennine Way, near the Nag's Head pub in Grindsbrook Booth. The route crosses sheep-fields and runs alongside a stream in torrent, then climbs to rough tussocky ground. It is not actually raining but the path is running with water, the footing slippy. Jim, who is leading, clasps a compass and map-case; he has told Tamsin that Kinder Plateau can be difficult in bad weather, and it looks like bad weather today. The clouds lower damply around them as they gain height. Jim walks to a steady rhythm, sure-footed, unlike some of the others who slip and grab at each other as they cross the stream. There is a steep bouldery scramble up a gully, a lot of puffing and a leg-aching climb, and they emerge on a plateau of black mud and rough grass.

Tamsin is not disappointed by the dismal weather, because she thinks it suits this wild scenery more than cloudless skies would. It is the strangest landscape she has ever seen. There are no trees, no bushes: just peculiarly liquid black peat, sedgy grass, crests and troughs, as remote and unfamiliar as the surface of the moon. The descending cloud hushes and muffles all sound. The soft ooze forms deep gullies, edged by drier peat in wave-like curls, appearing solid but giving way if stepped on and plunging the unwary walker into soggy blackness. Walking has become a matter of picking your way wherever it looks least treacherous and floundering through the deeper parts which clutch at boots and legs like quicksand. The Pennine Way, if they are still on it, is marked only by black footprints in the sludge. Tamsin can understand the difficulty in route-finding, especially in mist, since the dips and gullies make it difficult to keep any sense of direction. However, Jim seems to know where he is going, and eventually the straggling party arrives at a natural amphitheatre on the edge of the plateau, where rock falls away into a static tumble of angled surfaces, like a frozen avalanche. Kinder Downfall. They stop here for lunch, perching on rocks and watching the mist close in rapidly beneath them, giving the eerie sense that you could step off the edge of the Downfall into empty space.

It's too damp and cold to linger for long. They set off again, heading farther to the north-west towards Mill Hill and the Snake Pass.

"Stay together, everyone." Whistler herds the group closer with sheepdog-like flanking movements. "It'd be easy for someone to stray off and get lost up here."

"OK, Mother Hen," Candida mocks.

"As the only mature adult here," Whistler retaliates, "I feel a sense of responsibility for all you reckless young things."

"Thanks. We'll have your pipe and slippers ready when you get back."

Later in the afternoon, taking a different route by a rocky descent called Jacob's Ladder, they are rewarded by brief partings of the cloud which give glimpses of the valley: velvet green paddocks divided by stone walls, stunted trees clustering by the stream, a patch of hillside floating green-gold in a shaft of light. With no need to hurry, they linger on the way down, stopping to drink stewed coffee from their flasks, stringing out across the meadow from Grindsbrook Booth back to the hostel, which looks remote and superior on its perch above the hamlet, with wisps of cloud clinging to its roofs. For the last mile or so, Tamsin falls into conversation with Whistler and Fiona, who are thinking of walking the West Highland Way when Fiona has finished her finals. Tamsin feels relaxed, with the sense of well-being that follows strenuous exercise, pleased at having accomplished her first testing walk without disgracing herself by getting left behind. She can look forward to tomorrow. She is one of the group now.

Back at the hostel they pile into the drying-room and festoon the rails with damp clothing, and then make vast pots of tea in the self-catering kitchen. A little later, showered and tidied, they gather in the dining-room to queue for their supper. Walking makes you ferociously hungry, Tamsin realises. There is shepherd's pie, chips, vegetable bake for vegetarians; good sustaining stuff full of carbohydrates.

At her table, the talk is all of future trips.

"Who's for the Lakes then, last weekend in November?" Whistler asks. "I don't mind driving, if we can get the minibus."

"Which hostel are we staying at?"

"Not hostels, the bunkhouse near Keswick. Self-catering. I'll book it on Monday if enough people want to go." Whistler takes a notebook and pencil from his breast pocket and writes down *Lake District Weekend, November*.

"You can put me down," Dave says. "There might even be some snow by then."

"Fiona, myself." Whistler starts listing names.

"I don't know," Jane says, sighing. "It's really time I got down to some *work*."

"So should we all. Keep work in its proper place, that's my motto," Louise says cheerfully. "You can always catch up over Christmas. Put me down, Whistler. Cand?"

"Yeah, why not."

"What about you, Tamsin?" Louise asks.

"Yes, please." Tamsin likes Louise, who seems to want her to feel part of the group. Besides that, she has found that she can use Louise to measure her own capabilities. Louise is fairly short, with plump legs which hamper her over the stiles; Tamsin feels that if Louise can manage the ascents and scrambles and keep up with the group, then so can she. She feels less warm towards Jane, whose aloof manner is far less welcoming. Jane and Candida often withdraw together in gossipy conversations which exclude everyone else.

"Tamsin – is that with an s or a z? – thanks." Whistler writes her name down, followed by *Scott, Jim, Andy, Jon.* "That's enough to be going on with. We're in business."

Dave wants to do some winter rock-climbing, and is trying to persuade Jim and Scott to organise a trip for a more select group. He is muscular and athletic, with a weathered face, and gives the impression that today's outing has been no more exacting than a stroll to the pub. His remarks are scattered with references to buttresses, ice-pitches, and climbs with names like Needle Ridge and Hell's Groove. Jim looks interested, although he says, "I don't know, just yet. There's already this Glencoe trip after Christmas and then the Alps at Easter. I'm a bit pushed for cash, and besides I'm going to have to put in some time on my dissertation."

Dave turns his attention to Glyn instead. Dismayed by his talk of Mild Severes and horizontal traverses, Tamsin says in an undertone to Louise, "It won't be like that on the Lake District weekend, will it?"

"God, no," Louise says. "I wouldn't be going if it was. I mean, it'll be a lot steeper and ridgier than today – it depends on where they decide to go, and the weather. But you can always do an easier walk if you think you won't like it."

Tamsin wakes next morning to the sound of rushing water from the stream behind The Edges, and gentle breathing from the other bunks. She stirs, and the muscular ache in her legs reminds her how unfit she is for this kind of walking, in spite of the regular swimming. She walks painfully down to the showers and spends a long time under the needling hot water, feeling looser and refreshed. Dressed in her underwear she emerges from the steamy cubicle to find Candida standing naked on the carpet, towelling herself. Tamsin hasn't put her contact lenses in yet but she can see that Candida has a body to match her striking looks, small-waisted with full hips and breasts, her mane of hair falling springily to her shoulder-blades. Tamsin immediately feels prissy for having dressed in the privacy of her cubicle. She and Candida have hardly spoken more than two words to each other so far, and Candida's plainly evaluative stare makes her feel uneasy. She is about to make some trivial remark about whether it's likely to rain today when Louise bursts in to ask, "Did you bring any Tampax, Cand? Just my luck . . ."

"No, you'll have to try the shop."

"I've got some," says Tamsin, always prepared. She pulls on her jeans and T-shirt and goes upstairs with Louise to fetch them.

"How long have you been going out with Jim, then?" Louise asks on the way.

"It's not like that." Tamsin wishes the subject

didn't cause so much general interest; she wouldn't want to be labelled as Jim's girlfriend, even if it were true. If she's going on trips like this, she wants to go as one of the group, not as someone Jim's brought along.

But as soon as she is outside and walking, she forgets to care what Louise and the others think. Fiona and Whistler are leading today's walk, in a wide circuit taking in Lose Hill, Mam Tor and Rushup Edge. Although it isn't as high as Kinder Scout, there are better views today, down to farm and sheep-field, lane and stream. Cloud shadows shift along the valley floor where the deep reds and rusts of autumn glow in hazy sunshine. Tamsin is exhilarated, her stiffness gone, her spirits high with the scudding cloud. On Rushup Edge Jim waits for her, and they look across towards Kinder Plateau, smooth and benign in the sunlight. It looks an impressively long distance away, when Tamsin considers that they have covered the intervening miles on foot. Jim's shadow and her own are thrown uneven and elongated on the rough ground; the clocks have just gone back for winter and the sun is setting early.

"I wish we had another day or two," Tamsin says, thinking of city traffic and dirty streets.

"You're enjoying it?"

"It's great," Tamsin says. "I'm glad you told me about the spare place."

"It wasn't just a matter of making the numbers

up," Jim says. "I wanted you to come. And the Lake District will be even better."

They talk all the way back, intent on their conversation, letting others overtake them, so that when they find themselves on the zig-zag path up to the hostel Candida says scathingly, "Jim trailing behind? Never thought I'd see the day. You must be getting past it."

SCARECROW

Coming back from swimming on Monday morning, Tamsin hurries to answer a ringing telephone in the foyer of E.T. "Can I speak to Josie Franklin, please?" a female voice says, "Room 212?"

"Hang on a minute. I'll see if she's up," Tamsin says, doubting it. She runs upstairs two at a time and thumps on Josie's door.

"Come in," Josie's voice answers sleepily.

Tamsin pushes the door open so that she can stick her head in; she knows how easily Josie falls back to sleep if you only shout through the door. "Phone call for you . . ."

"What?" Josie says, stirring. It is dim inside with the curtains closed, but Tamsin sees that there is someone in bed with Josie, their bodies pressed together in the narrow space. The room is warm and stuffy with intimacy.

"Phone call, downstairs," she repeats, hearing her voice stiff with embarrassment. Josie's bed-mate raises his head and blinks, recognisable by his Rudolf Nureyev bone structure as Tibor. Tamsin goes out quickly, closes the door behind her and retreats to her own room. Don't they *mind* people walking in on them? A few moments later she hears Josie come out, yawning, and go padding off down the corridor in her slippers. Anyone telephoning the hall of residence has to be patient, and prepared for large phone bills.

Later, Josie treats it as a joke. "Honestly, Tam, you should have seen your face!" she teases. "You looked like a Victorian spinster who's just found the housemaid rutting with the stable-boy. I'd no idea you were such a prude!"

"I'm not!" Tamsin objects.

"It's not the first time Tibor's stayed the night."

"It doesn't matter to me who stays. It's up to you," Tamsin insists. "But letting me walk in like that – it could have been *anyone* –"

Josie shrugs. "So what? Everyone does it."

No, everyone doesn't, Tamsin thinks. She is familiar with the word *everyone* as a term to exclude rather than embrace: *everyone, except you. Everyone normal.* It is a familiar taunt from her school days, used to bribe parents or to emphasise membership of the in-group. In her class in Year 11 there was a bunch of sophisticates who paraded their sexual experience, wearing love-bites as badges of status, insignia to show membership of a club for the worldly-wise, the initiated. They would display the bruises like trophies, or would make a big show of covering them up with scarves or polo-necks, with much giggling and discussion of the reason for concealment to make sure that no one could avoid noticing. *Oh, come on, Tamsin, everyone does it.* Tamsin didn't. She would go home early from parties to avoid the stage where couples started fondling each other ostentatiously or disappearing into bedrooms. Physical intimacy without involvement was pointless, as far as she could see – merely aping the writhing bodies and the ecstatic faces of the cinema screen. And yet emotional intimacy was precisely what she feared. When she went out with boys from school it was always on a casual basis; she would break off as soon as anyone became intense or demanding.

"What's happened to Matthew/Chris/Richard?" Abigail would ask at intervals.

"Oh, I'm not going out with him any more," Tamsin would say.

"Pity. He seemed a nice boy."

"He's all right."

They were all nice boys, nothing objectionable about any of them, but whether or not she continued to go out with them had never mattered very much. This time (if there *is* a this time, she's still not sure) she thinks it might matter, more than she likes.

She sorts out what she will need for the day, her folders, notes, pens and pencils, instruments. Instead of thinking only about the day's lectures and lab activities she is wondering, and rather despising herself for it, whether she will see Jim today. There must be something the matter with her. In the bath last night, in bed, and swimming her lengths this morning, she found herself thinking of his laugh, his tall figure walking easily ahead of her, the way their eyes meet as if something is understood between them. She hasn't planned for this sort of thing and is amazed to find her thoughts running in so uncharacteristic a direction. Maybe she's got it all wrong; perhaps there's nothing special about it. Jim likes lots of people and lots of people like him; he is good-natured and unassuming and friendly. Seemingly uncomplicated, which Tamsin finds a definite attraction. She is the one who always looks for complications and difficulties.

But she doesn't really think she is mistaken. They have discovered some shared tastes besides the walking – they both detest Tory party politics, they have both read *Fools of Fortune* and seen *Howards End* – but it is more than that. She can't define what it is about him that makes her feel this; it isn't apparent from anything he has said or done, but from the way he *is*.

How can she be thinking like this about someone she's only just met?

Her mother's experience ought to make warning bells jangle, but Tamsin doesn't feel inclined to take notice, just now.

* * *

She doesn't see Jim that day, but on Tuesday afternoon she hears from him in an unexpected way when she logs on to the computer network to type up her lab report. After typing in her identity and password, she looks away to sort through her handwritten notes, and it is Tatsuya, working at the next terminal, who points out, "Someone's left you a message. Look."

She looks up at the screen, which reads **You have one new mail message**.

"Oh!" Tamsin says, childishly excited. She selects MAIL and READ, and the message comes up on the screen. She and Tatsuya read together:

The Collected Electronic Mailings of J. McGrath
Volume 1, part 1.
Are you coming walking on Sunday?
Will I see you before then? How about tonight?

Tamsin is pleased until she notices that the message was left yesterday. "Oh no!" She points. "Look at the date! It was here yesterday and I didn't see it."

"Presumably J. McGrath, whoever he is – I assume he's a he? – must realise that's one of the drawbacks of this rather oblique approach," Tatsuya says. "An unread communication isn't a communication."

"What do I do now?" Tamsin can't remember the procedure for replying, but Tatsuya is sure to know.

"That depends on whether you want to see him or not," he says.

"No, I mean about sending a message back."

"You just type your reply underneath, and press SEND."

Tamsin types:

1. **Yes**
2. **Yes, if you don't mind me turning up a day late. Where?**

Watching, Tatsuya says, "And here was I thinking you might come to the Christmas Dance with me."

Tamsin hasn't given the dance a thought. "Well, thanks, Tatsuya, but –"

"Your thoughts are engaged elsewhere, I can tell. Such is life," Tatsuya says stoically, returning to his keyboard.

Now that Jim has started it, sending messages by electronic mail becomes a regular habit. Each day that week Tamsin finds a message from him and sends one back, checking whenever she's near the study room. At first it's arrangements to meet: **See you in the library tonight, 8.30, at Gustave Klimt, Dewey 790.6?** Then Jim diversifies into silly jokes: **What do you call someone who used to be obsessed by agricultural machinery, but has got over it now?** he leaves for her one morning. Tatsuya is able to supply the answer, **An ex-tractor fan**, which Tamsin returns triumphantly in the afternoon.

By unspoken consent, they don't mention the

electronic conversations when they meet in person; it is another dialogue going on in the background.

Sunday is grey and dismal. Low cloud has been threatening all morning and as the group of walkers prepares to move off after lunch it starts to rain, a heavy sullen rain that looks set in for the rest of the day. Everyone scrambles into waterproofs, making each hooded figure indistinguishable from the next. Three or four people abandon the walk altogether, deciding to find the nearest pub and then catch a bus on to Bakewell. The others carry on, unwilling to admit defeat. Tamsin's waterproofs can't cope with driving rain; she is soon soggy around the shoulders, wrists and legs, but once she's got used to being damp she doesn't really mind. She has learned the way of it: you give yourself to the walk, the day, however bad the conditions, and press on to the end. In a way it is relaxing, because no matter how many essays or deadlines you have hanging over you, you can't do anything about them now. There is even a kind of perverse pleasure to be found in bad weather, sloshing on regardless of mud, puddles, slippery roots, clinging brambles.

Eventually, they trail into Bakewell in an unremitting downpour. In the dusk, lit shop windows offer warmth and dryness. Bakewell is open for tourists, and slow-moving parties crowd the pavements beneath a shuffling canopy of umbrellas.

"There's an hour to wait for the coach," Louise says, flipping back a sodden cuff to look at her watch. With so little temptation to linger along the way they have finished the walk sooner than expected. Scott and most of the others have already dispersed.

"Tea," Candida says firmly.

Louise looks across the road to an enticing tea-shop. An elderly group is being marshalled inside, shaking out umbrellas and examining wet footwear before funnelling through the doorway. "We'll never get in one of these dainty cafés," she points out, "not with pensioners' outings everywhere."

"Anyway, we can't trail all over their smart carpets. Look at the state of us," Tamsin says, looking down at their mud-clodded boots and overtrousers.

"There must be some greasy dive in a back street," Jim suggests, "even in Bakewell."

They roam damply around the town until they find a plastic-and-juke-box café near a lorry park. Leaving their boots, packs and wet gear inside the door they flock to the self-service counter and slump into chairs round a formica-topped table, clasping their hands around hot mugs of tea. They relax in the warmth and steam gently.

"We must be mad," Candida says. Her hair has sprung out into corkscrew curls, misted with rain. "It's your fault, Louise. You shouldn't have talked me into coming. I've got an essay deadline to meet."

"It's a bit late to start grumbling now," Louise says, ever-stoical.

"At least it'll help get me fit for skiing," Candida says, "otherwise it would have been a completely wasted day."

Louise is examining her wallet. "Look! Soaked through!" She flaps a limp five-pound note, lays it out to dry and then takes out a wad of soggy cardboard.

Candida leans over to look. "What's that?"

"Christmas Dance tickets," says Louise. "I brought them along to sell, but I forgot about them till now."

"Special reduction for flood damage?" Jim suggests.

Louise shakes her head and starts to peel off the tickets, layer by layer. "Come on then, Jim. Cough up."

"Oh, I don't know," Jim says. "I don't much like formal affairs, getting dressed up like a penguin."

Candida looks at him with a slow intimate smile. "You didn't mind last year."

"No. But that was last year," Jim says, rather curt. "I suppose you'll be going along to parade your latest catch?"

"Of course," Candida says smoothly. "What are dances for?"

"I don't know. That's why I probably won't go," Jim says.

They are getting at each other over something.

Tamsin doesn't know what, but she can tell that Louise is aware of it; her quick eyes dart from Candida's face to Jim's and back again. "If you've got any spare admirers, Cand," Louise says brightly, "pass one my way, will you? I haven't got anyone to go with yet. I bet I'll end up behind the bar again, like last year."

"I'm sure Jim will do the decent thing if you twist his arm," Candida says, seeming to ignore Tamsin deliberately.

"Do you want one, Tamsin?" Louise asks, proferring a soggy ticket.

"Perhaps," Tamsin hedges. "But I haven't got enough money on me."

Candida starts telling Louise about her Christmas skiing holiday, and Tamsin and Jim resume their conversation about walking in Ireland. Shortly, Candida gets to her feet and says, "We're going to the Bakewell tart shop. But don't let us interrupt your tête-à-tête." She does not so much leave as make an Exit, followed by Louise, who pulls an apologetic face behind her back as they stop in the doorway to pull on their boots.

"What's all that for?" Tamsin asks when the door has clanged to behind them. "She seems a bit spiky."

"Don't take any notice of her." Jim looks uncomfortable. "She's often like that. With me, anyway."

"Why?"

"Because I used to go out with her."

There is a pause, during which Tamsin is annoyed with herself for minding. Of course Jim has had girlfriends before; it would be ridiculous to suppose otherwise. But Candida . . . She remembers the conversation sleepily overheard at Edale and wonders how she can have been so gormless as not to have guessed.

"Was it a long-term –" Tamsin rejects *romance* and *relationship* and settles lamely for " – thing?"

"The whole of one term. Her first term, this time last year. I think she latched on to the first reasonable bloke who came along while she found her way around, but she soon got fed up with me once she realised she could attract anyone she wanted. I don't go skiing or drive a fast car or go to smart nightclubs, which is what her tastes run to. But the way she behaves sometimes you'd think I'd given her the push, instead of vice versa."

"Why does she still mind about it, then?"

"I don't think she does," Jim says. "It's an act with her. She loves to be the centre of attention, and she usually is – well, you can imagine. She likes to leave a trail of victims in her wake. She'd ditched me but I was supposed to be devastated about it for ever after. I was, at first."

Tamsin can't think what to say. Perhaps she has been mistaken; Jim is only using her to console himself for Candida. In which case she cannot possibly compete, and doesn't want to.

"I don't mean – well –" Jim says awkwardly.

"I suppose I was knocked sideways by Candida at first; anyone would have been. She's two years younger than me but she seemed older – her background's so different from mine, she's been everywhere and done everything. And when we split up, it wasn't just that she rejected me, but the way she did it – making it quite obvious that she didn't care in the least, turning up everywhere I went with different blokes in tow. She's quite conspicuous."

"Yes," Tamsin says. All the time he has been talking, her eyes have been fixed on the blue squares of the table-top, the sticky rings left by mugs, the spilled grains of sugar, as closely as if she is going to do a scale drawing from memory. Now Jim turns towards her and lifts a hand to stroke her damp hair and then her cheek. He is smiling, looking quite cheerful and normal, not in the least forsaken or broken-hearted.

"Look, I'm not making a very good job of this, am I? I don't want you to think I'm still drooping around the place like a jilted Elizabethan lover. Candida's a bit irritating at times, that's all. But it doesn't matter. Especially not now."

In the middle of the night, Tamsin wakes with the dizzy shock of not knowing where she is, her heart thudding, the shadows of a dream flickering just out of reach. Slowly, the curtained shape of the window comes into focus and she realises that she is in her own room in E.T. The building is completely silent, but she can still hear the echo of a voice from her dream. She focuses her mind on it, trying to recall the reason for her fright. "I've come to find you," it says, in a toneless, characterless voice. "I'm your father." There is a shape standing with its back to her, the shape of a tall man dressed in jeans and a grey sweater, and she is waiting and waiting for him to turn round so that she can see his face. And then he does turn, very slowly, to reveal a faceless blank, an empty disc, as round as a full moon, or a pumpkin. Her father is a scarecrow, mocking her. A scarecrow in Jim's clothes.

She thinks she understands now, though she didn't at the time, why her mother panicked once in Sainsbury's.

Tamsin, aged about five, was with her. Mum's trolley was half-full of bread, washing-powder, tins, packets, all boring things, and now she was choosing and weighing fruit and vegetables where they were laid out temptingly, a multi-coloured harvest. Tamsin reached out a hand to pick a black grape, dusty with bloom, and Mum said, "Don't touch, Tamsie. Not till we get home." It was always like that in the supermarket, looking at all these things she would like to touch, unwrap, eat, play with, but she wasn't allowed to. Once, she thought she was helping the shop ladies by moving a whole row of tins into an empty space, and couldn't understand why Mum started apologising to a cross lady in an overall and moving everything back with quick ashamed hands. It wasn't fair: grown-ups were allowed to pick up the grapes, so she couldn't see why she got told off. Now she was tired, but she was too big to ride on the trolley like she used to.

There were other people around her, reaching out, squeezing tomatoes, selecting mushrooms and putting them into bags, weighing things at the scales. She was used to that, dodging between the legs and the trolleys to find Mum, but suddenly she was aware of a tension, a strangeness. Mum was tight-faced, her eyes sliding, frightened, as if all the other people had become dangerous. She had been putting apples into a plastic bag but now she suddenly dumped them back on the pile instead of putting them into her trolley.

"Come on. We're going now," she whispered, bending down to Tamsin.

"But we haven't got the Sugar Puffs or the –"

"Shh. Shh! Don't talk. We've got to go. Hold on to the trolley and don't let go."

The checkouts were all busy with people unloading loaves, tins of cat food, packs of toilet rolls, which slid past the bored faces of the checkout ladies. Mum didn't want to wait. She pulled the trolley first in one direction, then another, then shoved it to one side of the aisle and left it, full of all the things she had spent so long choosing. She grabbed Tamsin's hand so hard that Tamsin thought she had done something wrong and was being punished. Tamsin started to wail.

"Shh, shh, Tamsie. Please!" Mum sounded as if she was going to cry too, or scream. She pulled Tamsin past the checkout, past the people waiting patiently with their trolleys and purses. Faces were staring at them, and a voice complained about being jostled.

"Here! Do you want all this stuff, or not?" an assistant yelled after them.

But the automatic doors were opening to let them out into the street. Mum was hurrying, grasping Tamsin's hand so hard that it hurt. They were almost running along the pavement, dodging mothers with prams and old people with tartan trolleys. Tamsin wondered if the cross man who had shouted out would run after them, make them go back and finish their shopping and pay for it. Or perhaps he thought Mum had stolen something. Tamsin was sobbing with shock and bewilderment. She had never seen her mother so frightened before.

Is Jim like her father? Is that why she feels she has known him before? Questions repeat themselves insistently in her head while she swims lengths in the almost-empty swimming pool. Reach, grab the bar, turn, push off, face underwater, the chlorine washing and stinging her eyeballs, slivers of light flashing and sliding beneath her as she launches into the next length, settling into the rhythm. Her muscles are still tight from the weekend's walk, making her slow to get going this morning . . .

At home a few months ago, someone on the radio said, "A young woman may often find herself unconsciously attracted to a man who resembles her father." Abigail, doing the ironing, gave an outraged *hmph*, looking at Tamsin, her glance clearly saying, Not in your case, I hope. At the time Tamsin found it more amusing than worrying, not thinking it at all likely. But is that what's happening now? Was her dream telling her as much? There is no point any more in trying to pretend that she isn't falling for Jim in a big way (*falling? knocked sideways?* Why do the conventional phrases suggest sinking and collapse, she wonders? It feels more like being elevated, uplifted) but it is happening almost in spite of her; it is a choice that has made itself. Unconscious it would have to be, more like telepathic, if she is looking for a father-substitute; she has never seen so much as a photograph of Paul Strivener. But no amount of brain-trawling can reveal where she might have seen Jim before, or who he reminds her of, and she can think of no other explanation but the one she doesn't want: that he is like her father.

Her lengths completed, she washes her hair in the shower, the herbal scent of the shampoo mixing with chlorine. She squeezes out the thick rope of her hair and sends floes of lather coursing down her body, the body that is half made up of genes from a complete stranger. She will have to find out, she decides; it is more than just curiosity now. This time she is going to persevere until she meets her father.

She leaves an E-mail message for Jim:

Do you know a man called Paul Strivener?

Jim's message comes back: **No. Who is he?**

Someone I've never met, she replies.

That's a funny coincidence then, Jim sends back. **Neither have I.**

She does not usually write letters to her mother – she has never before had any reason to – but this isn't something she feels she can discuss over the telephone, within earshot of anyone who might walk past.

Dear Mum,

You're not going to like this, but I have been thinking about it for a long time and decided that I really do want to try to track down my father, and meet him. I don't expect to like him after the way he treated you, and obviously he can't have the slightest interest in either of us or he would have made contact himself by now, but I do want to see him for myself even if it's only once. I hope you won't mind too much –

But Mum will mind, she knows that. She pictures her mother reading the letter, alone with her breakfast coffee, and knows that she can't it seems like defecting to the enemy, threatening Mum's peace of mind. She can't send a letter like that the day after her regular weekend checking-in phone call, out of the blue.

She rips the page from her notepad and chucks it into the bin. It occurs to her that perhaps she can find her father on her own, without telling anyone. Abigail can hear about it afterwards, and then there will be no need for her to worry.

LUXURY FLOORINGS

Now that Tamsin has planned her campaign, there seems no point in waiting any longer. Next day at lunchtime, collecting a sandwich instead of going to the refectory with Rikayah and the others, she goes to a public telephone box in the city centre. She feels furtive leaving the campus, as if she's doing something underhand, which in a way she is. If her first line of enquiry fails she will have to contact the college where her mother and father met, but it might be easier than that: Strivener isn't a common name, and she knows that Paul was living in Stevenage in the seventies. Unless his parents are ex-directory or have moved away, this stage could be straightforward.

She rings Directory Enquiries and the recorded voice obligingly responds: "The number you require is . . ." She writes it down, with a shaking hand. The next bit will be harder.

She sorts out change, feeds in 10p and keys in the Stevenage number, her heart thumping. The ringing tone sounds again and again into an un-responding blank. They might be out; she will have to try again this evening. Just as she is about to give up, she hears the click of the receiver being lifted, and then a voice, female and out of breath.

"Is that Mrs Strivener?" Tamsin asks.

"That's right, speaking."

"Hello. I'm an old friend of Paul's," Tamsin lies, "from when he was at art college. We're organising a reunion and I'd like to get in touch with him. I heard he'd gone to live in Cleveland – is he still there?"

"No, dear," Mrs Strivener says unsuspiciously. There is a suggestion of creaking and shuffling at her end, as if she's settling into a chair. Her voice is comfortable, homely, making Tamsin think of Yorkshire pudding on Sunday, washing on the line, family photograph albums by the TV. She pictures Mrs Strivener as overweight, with permed hair and fluffy slippers, and then realises with a shock that this is her grandmother. Her other grandmother. How would she respond if the next words were, "I'm your son's illegitimate daughter"?

Mrs Strivener continues, "No, he's in Birmingham now. Been there a couple of years. I'm not sure he's going to be all that keen on college reunions though. He put all that arty stuff behind him when he went to work with his dad. You an artist then?"

"Er . . . graphic designer." Tamsin has almost forgotten her alias. "Does he work in Birmingham?"

"That's right, dear. Carpet salesman. Works in Luxury Floorings, a big place near New Street Station. You want his address then? Got a pen handy?"

"Yes, thanks." Tamsin writes it down. "Is he married?"

"Oh yes, dear. Getting on ten years now. You *are* a bit out of touch then, aren't you?"

"We haven't had a reunion before," Tamsin says hastily. She doesn't like to push her luck by asking any more questions. She thanks Mrs Strivener for her help and rings off, leaning rather dizzily against the side of the kiosk until she realises that someone else is waiting for the phone. All this time, all the time she's been wondering and worrying, the information she needed was at the end of a two-minute phone call.

What now? She has her father's address and phone number, but she is wary of turning up there, or even of telephoning; Paul's wife may not know he has a daughter. Maybe he has a family. Tamsin would like to know, but she doesn't want to find out that way. The mention of Luxury Floorings was a bit of luck – better to contact him there. My father's a carpet salesman in Birmingham, she thinks, remembering childish fantasies in which he appeared as explorer, artist, musician.

She was only the carpet salesman's daughter, but she wasn't going to be floored ...

She wanders back to the campus for her afternoon session. She and Rikayah are surveying the campus water-gardens with a theodolite, taking measurements for a scale drawing. She stands holding the red-and-white pole, lost in thought, until Rikayah says, "Are you asleep, or what? I might as well do it all by myself."

Only once did Abigail talk seriously about Paul, telling Tamsin how it happened.

"I fell in love, or thought I did. I'd have done anything he wanted. I thought he was the best thing that had ever happened to me, or ever would. Love can be like that," Abigail said cynically. "People talk a lot of rubbish about how wonderful it is, but really it's more like temporary madness. Paul was an artist, or at least pretending to be – he was older than me, he'd had lots of girlfriends, he didn't care about passing exams, doing well for yourself, the sort of thing I'd been brought up to care about. I was at the rebellious stage when everything my mum and dad said and did seemed stuffy and repressive. We were having rows all the time at home. When Paul suggested going away together, it sounded so marvellous – freedom, away from our parents, no responsibilities, just ourselves. I was so naïve that it didn't occur to me that you've *got* to have responsibilities – you've got to eat, you've got to live somewhere and pay bills. But it was summer and we were going to live by the sea and we didn't think like that. We were going to be artists and it would be idyllic. I was too besotted to see what Paul was really like. He'd done a year of Art Foundation because it sounded good and he couldn't think what else to do, but he was too idle to pursue it, or pursue anything else for that matter. He was a drifter, looking for an easy ride through life. I can see why he impressed me so much at first, but I don't know how I didn't realise sooner that it was all one way. Of course it's easy to say that now. But I didn't even stop to think of the effect it would have on Mum and Dad and Rachel, clearing off without even leaving a note. When I got pregnant I didn't dare go home – I dreaded them knowing. I should have known Paul wouldn't be any use. As far as he was concerned it was *my* fault, not *our* fault. He wanted nothing to do with it. I should have known he'd do a bunk. The whole thing terrified him, but *he* didn't have to face the consequences. I did. It was only when I got pregnant that I started to grow up."

Tamsin listened in silence. It was hard not to believe that it was somehow her fault, for being conceived when no one wanted her, for driving her father away.

Abigail looked at her and smiled. "I got it all wrong, anyway. He wasn't the best thing that happened to me. You are."

* * *

On Friday Jim sends an E-mail message: **Come to the Playhouse tomorrow night? They're doing** *Hedda Gabler*.

Sorry, I can't, she sends back. **I'd like to but I've got to do something else on Saturday and I might not be back in time.**

Shall I get a ticket just in case?

Better not, thanks, she returns. **I don't know how late I'll be.**

What's all the mystery?

I'll tell you about it on Sunday, she replies, hoping she will be able to. She cannot seriously contemplate Saturday night or Sunday. Saturday is a barricade, a dividing line in her experience: before and after she meets her father. It might be all for nothing anyway; she has decided to take a gamble on Paul working on Saturdays, even though it could easily mean a wasted and expensive train journey to Birmingham. It would be easier to telephone him at work first, but then he might refuse to meet her. She wants to keep the advantage of surprise.

Shortly before twelve she arrives at New Street Station and emerges from the modern concourse into Saturday morning busyness. People jostle past in pairs and groups, making her feel intensely alone, nervous, her throat tight and dry. She wanders along what seems to be the main street, letting herself be distracted by a bookshop, a shoe shop, an outdoor suppliers; there's a Gore-Tex coat in the window just like Jim's, provoking a thud of regret that she didn't ask him to come with her. But that would have been impossible. She must do this on her own.

Telling herself sharply to get on with it, she chooses a likely looking passer-by to ask for directions. She hasn't come to Birmingham to look in shop windows.

The carpet shop turns out to be in the other direction, back past the station. The window is full of imitation Persian rugs, and plain wool carpets at special offer prices, huge strips of them fanned out in a spectrum of discreet colours. She walks slowly into the atmosphere of cut wool and rubber underlay, past tall pillars of carpeting. A few salesmen stand about, but they are far too young to be her father, in their early twenties at the most, in aggressively cut suits and red ties and slick hairstyles. They are about Jim's age but a different species altogether.

One of them comes smartly over to her. "Can I help you at all?"

"I'm looking for Mr Strivener. Is he here today?"

"He'll be in Kitchen and Bathroom Flooring, Upper Sales Floor."

Tamsin goes up, fighting an urge to run away and forget the whole thing. She is almost there, she has done it, he's here on this floor and her search has been successful, but her knees threaten to give way and she clutches at the hand-rail for support. Her eyes swivel frantically around the upper floor, her contact lenses blurring over. The next person she sees could be her father. There is a plump fiftyish man with a sweaty face and a thin moustache, showing carpet swatches to a customer – no, that *can't* be him. Another man, younger, with curly brown hair, is sitting at a desk humming and filling in forms. She approaches, swallowing with difficulty. He looks up at her and she knows at once that this must be her father. It isn't Jim's face after all that she recognises, but oddly assembled elements of her own.

He stops humming and smiles. "Yes? Can I help you?"

She tries to control her voice. "Mr Strivener?"

"That's right," he says, and she sees that he is wearing a lapel badge: Paul Strivener, Sales Manager.

"I'm your daughter," she says.

In spite of her agitation she watches his reaction closely, as if conducting an experiment. He half-stands, then sinks back into his chair; his face slowly reddens, with staring eyes. He tries to speak but the words are choked off in his throat.

"You're . . . you're . . ." he falters, shaking his head as if that will make her disappear. He blinks rapidly and tries again. His eyes are blue-grey, exactly the same as hers. "Christ Almighty, you are, aren't you." It's a statement, not a question. "You're the spitting image of her – of Abby. It's like seeing a ghost."

"My mother's not dead," Tamsin says tightly.

Paul Strivener glances furtively at the plump man, who is still busy with his customer. Tamsin can almost see the questions forming themselves like cartoon thought bubbles: *How did you find me? Where have you come from?*

Instead, he says, "What do you want?"

His eyes are narrowed, suspicious, and it occurs to Tamsin that he thinks she's here to threaten or blackmail him.

"I don't want anything," she says. "Only to see my – my father."

"Well, here I am." He relaxes a fraction, giving a nervous laugh. "Christ, this is peculiar, isn't it?"

"Yes, I –" Tamsin isn't sure what to say next. Her imaginings have taken her this far, face to face with him, but not beyond. And she sees that he too has no idea what to say or do. If anyone's going to take control of the situation, it will have to be her.

"Are you going out for lunch?" she suggests. "Is there somewhere we could talk?"

"Yes, best idea," he agrees quickly. He would like to get her out of the store, Tamsin guesses, before anyone overhears. "Wait here a minute, will you?"

He goes over to speak to the plump man, and Tamsin hears the word "niece". She has become his niece, to save him embarrassment. She watches him walk back towards her, trying to see the young man who so impressed her mother that she left home and family to run away with him when she was younger than Tamsin is now. He is tall, well-proportioned, though a little podgy around the middle; he is, she realises, quite a handsome man, in a well-fed, well-groomed way. There is a suggestion of swagger in his walk; it is a city-dweller's walk, toes turned slightly outward, quite unlike Jim's distance-covering stride. Regaining his composure slightly he tugs at the lapels of his jacket, picks up a silver pen and slips it into his top pocket, then rests a hand on her shoulder, gesturing towards the staircase. He is a mature man in a suit, a man used to knowing what's what and getting things done, telling people what to do. He is in control now, showing her where to go, his manner suggesting that he is used to escorting women, making gallant little after-you gestures. Only he wasn't very gallant to Mum, Tamsin thinks. She wonders what he will say about it.

Downstairs, the young salesmen stare curiously, and she wonders whether they'll be given the niece story later. Paul doesn't speak until he gets outside, and then he turns to her with another edgy laugh and she realises that he isn't quite as controlled as his movements suggest. "There's this little Italian place I go to sometimes. Would that be OK? It's either that or the pub."

"The Italian place will be fine," Tamsin says. They walk along the pavement together, not speaking. Now that she is with her father for the first time in her life, she can't think what to say to him. He looks at her several times with a slight shake of his head as if he can't believe she's really there. I'm walking along the street with my father, my dad, Tamsin thinks, although she can't really convince herself. Paul Strivener is a complete stranger with a face that is oddly familiar.

Outside the restaurant he stops dead and stares at her. "You know, I don't even know what your name is?"

"It's Tamsin."

"Tamsin? Unusual name, that. Nice. Abby's choice?"

"Yes." Of course it was, she thinks. Who else had any say in the matter?

"And your surname?" he asks awkwardly.

"Well, Fox, the same as Mum's." She is surprised at his question until she realises that he thinks Abigail might have married and changed her name. "She's always been single."

Paul looks taken aback by this. He says no more and leads the way inside. Like the pub that thinks it's in Dublin, the restaurant is pretending to be in ancient Rome. The décor is all terracotta and white tiles, marble tables, and representations of garlanded Caesars which gaze haughtily over the heads of the lunching shoppers.

Paul guides Tamsin to a small corner table and sits down opposite. They are uncomfortably close. He leans forward, elbows on the table.

"Where have you come from? Is Abby still living in Hertfordshire?" He speaks in an undertone so that people at other tables won't be able to hear.

"She is, but I'm at university. I came down by train."

Paul rubs a hand over his eyes as if he still thinks she might disappear into thin air. "I suppose we've got an awful lot of questions to ask each other."

A waiter comes up and hands them a menu each. Tamsin waves hers away. She doesn't feel at all hungry, although she hasn't eaten anything yet today. "Nothing for me, thanks."

"Oh, go on. You ought to have something," Paul says, like a concerned parent. "The food's very good here, I can recommend it."

"Well, just a salad then," Tamsin concedes.

"You don't mind if I –? It's a long day."

"No, go ahead."

Tamsin studies him closely while he looks at the menu. His face is thin, with a bony nose and mobile, shapely mouth; his expression is stern in repose. His hair is thick and well-cut, shaved neatly in front of his ears. She finds herself mentally portioning out her own features: my eyes and nose came from him; my hair obviously came from Mum but my face shape is something like his . . . It feels peculiar to be thinking this about a complete stranger.

Paul orders the food and a bottle of wine, and then sits back in his chair and smiles at Tamsin across the table. Giving orders to the waiter seems to have restored his poise. His smile is self-consciously engaging, a boyish grin which starts with a tightening of the cheek muscles, the lips parting over irregular white teeth. It is a smile he uses to charm women, she guesses, uneasily aware that he is treating her as he would a woman his own age. She thinks of him in bed with her mother, kissing, touching. Telling her lies.

"Well, Tamsin, it's a bit of a shock, you turning up like this," he remarks.

She fiddles with her fork. "Yes, I suppose it must be." She feels more shocked than he seems, and unlike him she has had time to prepare herself.

"How did you find me here?"

She tells him of the phone call to his mother, and he sits forward anxiously. "You didn't say who you were?"

"No, of course not."

He puffs out his cheeks with relief and fans himself with one hand. "That would have stirred things up and no mistake. They don't know about you, my parents. And I'm glad you didn't turn up at home, either."

"Your wife doesn't know?" she guesses.

He shakes his head, tight-lipped. Tamsin is beginning to feel invisible: she is someone who doesn't exist, unnamed until five minutes ago, someone who has been tidied up out of the way. How has Paul lived with such a secret? Had he conveniently forgotten all about her, until she turned up to remind him of her existence?

"Have you got any children?" she asks, deliberately not saying *any other children*.

"No. We were going to – we both wanted them – but we couldn't have them. Funny how things work out, isn't it? We had to go through all those tests to see which one of us was, you know, sterile. And all the time I knew full well . . ."

Poor wife, Tamsin thinks.

"Couldn't you have adopted a baby?" she asks.

"Well, perhaps." He looks doubtful. "Anyway, tell me about yourself. So you're at university? You're quite brainy then? You didn't get that from me."

Tamsin tells him about her course. The food arrives: a crisp salad for Tamsin; for Paul, meat in a sauce that smells fragrantly of wine and herbs, with vegetables in a side dish. He pours out wine for both of them, lifts his glass and then pauses.

"Well! Here's to – here's to you, Tamsin. I must say I'm impressed. University, and Engineering – funny choice for a girl, isn't it?"

"No, not at all. It doesn't require physical strength."

"What sorts of things do you do then?"

She describes the course while they eat, although there are far more important things to talk about. She can only pick at her salad. When Paul's plate is cleared, she forces herself to say, "I want you to tell me about you and Mum. How you met, what happened."

He looks at her warily. "Abby must have told you. I bet she's told you I'm a right bastard."

This is accurate enough, but Tamsin says, "She doesn't talk about it much."

"And you've never had a step-dad?"

"No. There's just the two of us."

Paul pours out more wine. "And is she still gorgeous?"

Tamsin is amazed to hear a note of wistfulness in his voice, almost as though Abigail was the one who upped and left. "Yes. I suppose she is."

"I'm surprised she never got married. I'd have thought she'd always have blokes flocking after her."

"I think what happened with you might have put her off men," Tamsin says carefully.

"Yes. I suppose that wouldn't be surprising." Paul can't quite meet her eye. "Well, what was it like, you want to know . . . We were so young then, both of us, hardly more than children . . ."

She isn't going to let him evade responsibility so easily. "You were nineteen or twenty, weren't you? Older than I am, and I'm not a child."

"All right. Young and naïve, let me put it like that." He is turning his wine glass round and round on the table, looking at it rather than at Tamsin. "Both fed up with living at home, with rules and arguments. She was a stunning girl, Abby was, a real cracker, and knew it. It was summer, the seventies, that whole laid-back scene – God, it seems a lifetime ago now – and we had the chance of sharing a house by the sea with friends. It was too good to miss. We probably didn't think any further ahead than the next few weeks. Things like steady jobs, mortgages and the like were a long way off. Anyway, we were living together, and Abby was supposed to be going to the doctor's or the family planning clinic to, you know, go on the Pill. But she never got round to it, and the inevitable happened. As you know."

He looks up briefly. Tamsin sips her wine, not responding. He hasn't said anything about loving her mother. He talks as if Abigail had been a glamorous accessory.

He lowers his voice. "God, when I found out she was pregnant, I just panicked. I didn't know what the hell to do. So I took the coward's way out and cleared off. Well, you must know that much. I'm not very proud of it now, I can tell you, but at the time I just couldn't see a way out of it. Abortion was the only answer as far as I could see, but when I mentioned it to Abby she just about blew her top. I couldn't get her to see sense at all. That made me panic even more. I didn't want the responsibility. I was only nineteen, with my whole life ahead of me, just getting a taste of freedom – I couldn't let one mistake take all that away. So I did a bunk." He gives Tamsin a fleeting glance and then his eyes slide away from hers. His hands fidget with the paper napkin. "I can guess what you must be thinking. But to tell you the truth, I was dead scared she'd come after me, go knocking on my parents' door and make me marry her, or pay up. So I – well, I left her some money, hoping she'd come to her senses, and cleared off to France. I needed to be well out of the way. I hardly dared come back, I was so sure Abby's parents would have got on to mine, but to give her credit she kept it all to herself."

Tamsin stares at him, trying to take in the fact that she is having lunch with a man who wanted her life to end before it began. "So you never knew, till now, whether or not she actually went ahead and had the baby? She could have had the abortion for all you knew?"

"No, I did know." He looks at her directly. "I saw her once. Years ago now. I was visiting an old mate and I was in the supermarket picking up a few cans of beer when I saw her with a little kid – with you. She saw me, too. I didn't know whether to speak to her or not but I never got the chance, because the minute she saw me she shot off as if the hounds of hell were after her. She must have thought I was going to snatch you off her or something."

"I remember it," Tamsin says, although she doesn't think he believes her.

The waiter comes by to collect their plates. Paul looks relieved, now that he has told her. He offers dessert, which she refuses, then orders coffee for them both.

"You must hate me," he says when the waiter has gone. "I don't blame you if you do."

Tamsin looks down at her place-mat, unable to answer. She doesn't dislike him as much as she expected to. She feels less hostile towards him in this penitent mood than when he was being brash and confident in the shop, or when he was trying to charm her.

"Did you – did you love her, my mum?" she asks. It is important for her to know.

Paul's eyes meet hers briefly and he seems to think seriously before answering. He shakes his head slowly. "I don't think I did – not then. I took her for granted. But later I started to feel bad about leaving her in the lurch and that time started to seem like the best in my life. Living with Abby, parties on the beach, the long hot summer . . . You know, I'd like to see her again. How is she? Still living in Hertfordshire, you said?"

Tamsin has become increasingly alarmed by his tone. "She's fine," she says curtly.

"What does she do for a job?"

"She works in an insurance office. But that's not the main thing she does. She's an artist, a good one. She's had local exhibitions and sold quite a few pictures."

"Yeah?" Paul looks impressed. "I wonder if she'd – I wonder if I could get in touch? I'd like to see her again," he repeats.

"But what about your wife?" Tamsin says,

amazed. "I don't see how you *could* – and anyway I'm not giving you our address. Mum doesn't know I've come to find you and she'll be furious when I tell her. She hates you, don't you realise?"

"Does she? Well I'm not surprised." Paul looks almost pleased by this, and Tamsin realises that she has made a mistake: her mother might despise Paul, even fear him, but she does not hate him. Hatred is too strong an emotion, the other side of love. "I can't help wondering what might have happened if – well, you know." He shakes his head wistfully. "If I hadn't cleared off like that. Who's to say it wouldn't have been all for the best if Abby and me had made a real go of it? And it hasn't really worked out with Denise. It's not worked out at all well, if you want the truth. With no kids, on top of everything else."

Tamsin assimilates this. "Why did you get married?"

"I never should have done. I fell into it, too lazy to avoid it. It's a trap, marriage. Before you know where you are you've got bills, mortgages, peeling paintwork, mothers-in-law, the whole works. But no kids. That's what spoiled it for us. And now I find out I've got a lovely grown-up daughter."

Tamsin looks at him in dismay, not sure what he's getting at. "But you've always known that! It's no surprise to you."

"I know, but seeing you like this, out of the

blue –" He leans forward across the table as if he's about to take her hand, but she draws back quickly. "Listen, Tamsin – now that we've met, we'll stay in touch, won't we? I could easily come up to your university sometimes and take you out. It's not far on the motorway –"

"No!" Suddenly Tamsin has to get away. It's all going wrong. She fumbles in her wallet for money to pay for her meal and slaps it down on the table – she doesn't want to be under any obligation to Paul.

He reaches across the table again, his face alarmed.

"Wait! Don't rush off. I didn't mean to –"

Tamsin ignores him, getting to her feet and hauling on her coat. "I've got to go. I only wanted to know what you were like. And don't even *think* of getting in touch with my mother!"

People are listening, forks poised half-way to mouths, faces swivelling in her direction. Hardly knowing what she's doing, she stumbles over carrier bags and runs out into the street, making for the station in a headlong dash. She should have stayed invisible.

MISSING

*T*amsin goes with Jim to see *Hedda Gabler* after all. Actors move about in front of her eyes and voices wash over her; she makes only intermittent contact with the plot. Jim is engrossed, but he looks at her oddly now and then and she tries to make a better effort.

On the way back to campus he talks about the play. "I'm never sure whether we're expected to sympathise with Hedda or not. I mean, in some ways she's a sad character because of being so frustrated, but then she's chosen to marry someone she doesn't love, and when she burns the manuscript it's such a deliberately destructive thing to do. Getting back at Lövborg in the only way she knows . . ."

"Mmm," Tamsin says.

Jim looks at her closely. "Tamsin! Have you listened to a single thing I've said?"

"Yes. Sorry. Well, Hedda –" She tries to remember. "She had a lot of energy but didn't know what to do with it . . . I mean, she . . . well, you know . . ."

"Oh, never mind Hedda Gabler. It's obvious you haven't got a clue. And you still haven't told me where you went today. What's all the secrecy for? What's happened? You've hardly spoken to me all evening."

Tamsin can't help feeling uneasy about what she has done. The meeting with her father may have settled one kind of doubt but it has produced bigger and more urgent ones; it feels alarmingly like the start of something. It would have been simpler to find that she hated her father and could dismiss him from her thoughts for ever, but she can't – he is part of her now, more than just the provider of half her genes; he has invaded her mind. She isn't sure what he meant when he spoke about her mother in that nostalgic way. She should have left him alone. There are more people involved than just herself: Mum, Paul, Paul's wife. And she still hasn't answered Jim's question. They have come to a standstill, but now he walks on, hands thrust deep into his pockets and shoulders hunched. "Oh, never mind. I suppose you went to see some boyfriend. But it's none of my business. You don't have to tell me."

It hasn't occurred to her that he might misunderstand so completely. She hurries after him. "No, wait! It wasn't that at all! What happened was that I – went to find my father."

Jim stops abruptly. "You did what? How?"

"Met my father. I found out where he works and I went to see him."

She explains, as fully and as honestly as she can, all the way back to Jim's flat, which is in a Victorian terraced house close to the campus. Jim listens, occasionally asking a question but not commenting, and she feels even more strongly that she has done something irrevocable.

"I suppose it was a silly thing to do?" she appeals to him when they get indoors, watching him light the gas fire.

"I don't blame you though. I'd have done the same." Jim straightens, takes her coat and then stares at her in amazement. "What you said just now – you really thought I was your long-lost brother or something?"

"No! Not as literally as that. I thought my father must be like you, or you like him. There must be some reason why I thought I recognised you."

"There was. You recognised me as an overwhelmingly fascinating person."

"Ah, that must have been it. How silly of me not to realise."

He sits down on the battered sofa and pulls her close. Scott and Whistler are both out, and they have the place to themselves for a while. "Come here. I don't want to remind you of your father."

"You don't. Not any more."

* * *

By Monday lunchtime there is an E-mail message for Tamsin. She calls it up and reads: **Yeats knew how to put it –**

We sat under an old thorn-tree
And talked away the night,
Told all that had been said or done
Since first we saw the light,
And when we talked of growing up
Knew that we'd halved a soul
And fell the one in t'other's arms
That we might make it whole.

She smiles, imagining Jim searching through his books, reading, choosing. Yeats is his favourite poet, and he has chosen his favourite poet to explain. She loves his way of being more romantic by E-mail than he is in person.

Dear Nan, Tamsin begins. She stops and chews the end of her pen, knowing that she won't be able to mention any of the most important things that have happened recently.

Thanks for your letter and the newspaper cutting. I'm sorry I missed the exhibition but I'll be able to see Mum's pictures when I get home, except for the one she sold.

Not long now till the end of term. I'm looking forward to coming home for Christmas, but in between there are things going on here – a party on Saturday (for someone who's reached the grand age of twenty-one), a weekend in the Lake

District, and a Christmas Dance. This seems to be quite a grand affair, a bit like the Oxford balls Aunt Rachel told me about. It seems that the done thing is to go with a partner – yes, even in the liberated 1990s, girls wait coyly to be asked. I think I might wait a long time. The only partner I want is not at all keen on swanky evening bashes and would be far happier toiling up a mountain in pouring rain (which is probably what we'll be doing in the Lake District. I've noticed that any bunch of walkers, anywhere, immediately attracts thunderous cloudbursts – there must be some scientific principle behind it, as yet undiscovered). Also, poor little Cinderella doesn't have a thing to wear (for the ball, I mean, not for the Lake District). As I'm not often invited to the Oscar awards or film premières, spangly evening dresses don't form part of my wardrobe. So if I do go, I shall have to beg or borrow something.

My course is going well, although we are struggling with differential and integral calculus, even (especially, in some cases) the people doing straight Maths degrees. We are about to be initiated into the use of the Scanning Electron Microscope (SEM to those in the know). Yesterday, a post-grad student was supposed to be showing a group of us how to use it. He gave us a great spiel about what we would do and how and why, while we all stood there eagerly with our notepads. Then as soon as he turned it on there was a loud ping – the filament had gone. He dithered about for the next half hour trying to fix it, with us giving useless advice – of course there was no technician in sight. The poor bloke was getting more and more flustered, and redder and redder, while we all waited. I don't think he'd ever supervised undergraduates before and I felt quite sorry for him. Our session ended before he'd managed to sort it out, so the SEM is still a mystery.

I'll send you a postcard from the Lake District . . .

Sealing the letter and addressing it, Tamsin is very conscious that the voice she has used – jokey, jolly – is not her own. She doesn't talk like that, and wonders why she feels obliged to assume it whenever she writes to Nan. The things that really matter are left unsaid: *Dear Nan, I've met my father. Dear Nan, I think I'm in love. Dear Nan, please don't get ill and die.*

Nan, Tamsin remembers, has had her share of the family's bad luck with relationships. Nan has never mentioned it, but Grandad Charlie told Tamsin about it when she was doing a GCSE History project on the war.

The war had always been evident to Tamsin, in old photographs, songs, films. It was woven into her grandparents' conversation: *that was while we were in the air force . . . when we still had rationing . . . it was Make Do and Mend in those days . . .* It was almost a part of her own life, the day before yesterday rather than firmly in the distant past, familiar from classroom displays of Dig for Victory posters and maps of the D-Day landings, and from books she read as a child: *Carrie's War*, *Goodnight Mr Tom*, *The Exeter Blitz*. Compared to the horrors of the First World War, brought to life by the poems she read in English lessons, her grandparents' war seemed altogether more tolerable. The Home Front, to Tamsin, was people riding cheerily about on bikes or digging their potatoes, eating jelly at street parties and singing Vera Lynn songs.

But that view changed when Grandad Charlie talked to her about the bomber base in Lincolnshire where he and Nan met.

"Forty-three, forty-four, those were the worst years," he told her. "That was when I met your Nan. She was working in flying control. Three or four nights a week, twenty or so Lancasters would fly out over Germany and not all of them would come back. Every time a plane was lost, that was seven men killed. Sometimes they might have survived and been taken prisoner. We wouldn't have known. Chaps would be there one day and gone the next."

Tamsin couldn't imagine it. Once at school, a girl from another year had been killed in a cycling accident and the whole school had mourned; pupils went about with shocked faces and talked in hushed respectful voices. What must it have been like when people disappeared in sevens, night after night?

Grandad showed her his old photograph album, with pictures of himself in overalls and Nan in WAAF uniform. He pointed in turn at a moustached face beneath a peaked cap, a pilot waving from a cockpit, a grinning bunch of aircrew in flying gear. "This bloke, he won a DFC medal. He survived and worked as an instructor after the war . . . This one was lost on the Nuremberg raid in forty-four. This bunch are Canadians, good fun they were . . . They all died when their Lanc crashed in fog. All young blokes, nineteen, twenty or so, most of them . . ." He shook his head. "Such a terrible waste. Most of them didn't even expect to survive. The odds were one in twenty against you coming back each time. Doesn't sound too bad until you take into account they'd do fifty or sixty trips. Imagine facing that night after night."

"Didn't you want to fly, Grandad?"

"Couldn't pass the eyesight tests," Grandad said. "No, I was just a ground engineer. Probably wouldn't be here now otherwise."

"What's happening here?" Tamsin pointed to a group of people dressed up in costumes.

"That was one of our shows," Grandad said. "We did find time to have fun too. Just as well. There's Nan, look. And there's me with the donkey's head and big ears. We're in *A Midsummer Night's Dream*."

Nan's face looked out of the photograph, round-cheeked and girlish beneath a waved wartime hairdo which looked odd with the diaphanous Greek costume she wore.

"She was pretty, wasn't she? Tamsin said.

"Oh yes, she was a lovely girl, your Nan," Grandad Charlie said proudly. "I always had a soft spot for her, even when . . ." He flipped over the pages and stopped at a photograph of a young man: dark-haired, serious, looking as if he felt proud to be in RAF uniform.

"This chap here was your Nan's boyfriend when I first knew her. David, his name was; he was aircrew, a navigator. They were crazy about each other. You've seen that gold locket Nan always wears? That was a present from him."

"What happened?"

"He went missing," Grandad said. "March forty-four. No one ever knew what happened. His crew set off on a raid to Berlin and never came back. For a long time Nan hoped he was in a prisoner-of-war camp, even after his own folks had made their mind up he must be dead. Eventually she had to accept it. And after a while she married me."

Tamsin looked at the dark eyes of the young man in the picture and thought that perhaps she'd have been crazy about him too if she'd been around at the time. Of course Grandad Charlie was lovely too – it wasn't as if Nan had made do with second best – but in a quite different way.

"Don't you mind?" she asked him. "Nan wearing the locket someone else gave her?"

Grandad thought for a moment and then shook his head. "No. Not at all. She told him she'd always wear it, so if she didn't it would have been as if he'd never existed. We both knew so many that died. It's a way of remembering them. Like wearing a poppy on Remembrance Day."

Tamsin wrote down some notes for her project. The kind of work people did on the airfield; how many bombing raids there were and where to; the loss statistics. But foremost in her mind was the idea that Nan had loved someone else before Grandad, presumably would have married him if he had survived, but had lost him.

We are unlucky in our family, she thought. It has happened to all of them, my great-grandmother, Nan, Mum. No sooner do they love someone than he disappears. Our family is full of vanishing men, like a portrait gallery of ghosts.

I won't let it happen to me, she decided.

And soon after that conversation Grandad died, vanishing after the others.

Getting ready for the party on Saturday evening, Tamsin stares distrustfully at her face in the mirror. It doesn't quite seem to belong to her any more, now that she can see Paul Strivener in it. She feels as if the reflected face might take on his expression or speak to her in his voice, telling her that she can't run away and pretend she doesn't exist. Which is exactly what *he* did.

What has she done? Every morning she imagines him getting ready for work, putting on his smart suit and his business persona, saying goodbye to the wife he doesn't love and who doesn't know he is a father. Does he think about me, she wonders, while he sits at his desk ordering carpets and floor tiles? Does he feel different now that he has a real live daughter? And, just as important, does he think about Mum? Was he serious about wanting to see her again, or was that just a passing whim?

Tamsin recognises her mistake. Like a young child, she has taken it for granted that both parents, being grown-up, were long past thinking of new relationships or old desires. Her awareness that they are both under forty, both unusually attractive, and both dissatisfied with their present situations, nags unpleasantly at the edge of her brain. *Surely* not . . .

She decides that her hair will have to do, scowls at her reflection and tugs at the neck of her T-shirt, which is inclined to sag. It is time to call for Josie and go over to the flat.

Having been there a few times by now, Tamsin is used to the general clutter of three untidy males sharing – dishes piled in the sink, three-week-old newspapers scattered on the floor, socks drying on the radiators, books and half-written essays lying everywhere – but finds that for tonight everything has been tidied up and superfluous furniture moved to the landing above. Rock music thumps through the floorboards as she and

Josie climb the stairs, and she hopes the neighbours are tolerant. Scott, whose twenty-first birthday is the excuse for the party, looks fairly tanked-up already, and the flat is decorated with silly string, phallic balloons and cartoon pictures of Scott in various undignified or compromising positions.

"Who drew those?" Tamsin asks Jim.

"Whistler. He's dangerous with a pencil in his hand. If you ever see him looking your way, dive for cover."

The flat fills up. Most people present are second- or third-year students, apart from Tamsin, Josie, and Candida's new boyfriend, who turns out, much to Tamsin's amusement, to be the insufferable Toby from the engineering group.

"He's *awful*," she whispers to Josie. "Thinks he's God's gift to engineering and the world in general. But I suppose he meets Candida's requirements – a rich Daddy and his own car."

Tamsin cannot exactly like Candida, but Candida is at least pleasant towards her this evening, perhaps because Toby is in tow. "All ready for the Lakes next weekend?" she asks Tamsin. "I wonder if there'll be snow? I don't want to have to bother with crampons and ice-axe."

Tamsin feels herself turning pale. "Are you coming, Toby?" she asks, hoping not. Candida *and* Toby would be a bit much to take.

Toby looks appalled. "Good God, no. I don't

know what possesses people to go marching about in mud and rain. Sheer masochism. If I want to go up a mountain I take a ski lift. Besides, the Lake District hills are only pimples compared to the Alps or the Dolomites. Do you ski?" he asks Tamsin in his cocktail-party manner.

"No, I prefer pimples," Tamsin says, and Josie splutters into her drink.

Toby gives a no-accounting-for-taste shrug and follows Candida towards the drinks table.

"Where's Tibor tonight?" Tamsin asks Josie.

"No idea. We don't live in each other's pockets," Josie says. "And he doesn't know many of this lot. Neither do I really. It was Scott who invited me." Josie hasn't been out with the walking group since the Dovedale outing, partly through lack of inclination and partly because she is often involved in drama workshops or rehearsals at weekends.

"How's the play coming on?" Tamsin asks.

"Getting there. We're putting up the set tomorrow." The theatre group is producing *The Royal Hunt of the Sun*, and Tamsin is getting accustomed to Inca chants coming from Josie's room at odd hours.

"You and Jim seem to be seeing a lot of each other," Josie remarks chattily. She lowers her voice slightly. "Have you been to bed with him yet?"

"Shhh!" Tamsin hopes no one has overheard. Josie's openness about such things has the effect of making her clam up like an offended maiden aunt. She waits for Josie to tell her what a prude she is.

"Sorry, none of my business," Josie says, unabashed. "I keep forgetting what a sweet old-fashioned thing you are. Ready for another drink?"

"No, thanks." Tamsin holds up her half-full glass, and Josie goes over to the loaded drinks table, where she is waylaid by Scott. Left by herself, Tamsin thinks about the *yet*. It hasn't got to that stage with herself and Jim, and it's not going to be a topic for discussion with Josie or anyone else, but is it as inevitable as Josie seems to suggest? Tamsin is aware that although the prospect is a new one for her, it almost certainly isn't for Jim (she tries not to think too hard about Candida), and the situation is bound to arise sooner or later. Sooner, if their drawn-out late-night partings are any indication. Away from home, without parental disapproval or curfew hours, cohabiting is easy, perhaps *too* easy; there are no domestic rulings to provide a safety-net. But she doesn't feel prepared for so big a commitment yet; she is unwilling to rush into something so important, especially given her mother's disastrous example. She looks around for Jim. He clearly has other things on his mind at present: he is sitting cross-legged on the floor by the bookshelves with Dave and Glyn, studying maps and deep in conversation about their New Year trip to Scotland, while Whistler listens.

" – Bidean nam Bean's supposed to be spectacular – we might get a clear day if we're lucky." Jim's face is warm with enthusiasm. "We could go up from Meeting of the Waters, here, and take in Beinn Fhada and Stob Coire nan Lochan –"

"Yeah, I've done that before, but in summer," Glyn says. "It'd be fantastic in snow."

"And then we'd be well placed for a day on the other side of Glencoe. What's it called –" Dave takes the map.

"The Aonach Eagach," Glyn provides. "But the ridge can be quite exposed in bad weather. I wouldn't fancy it in high wind or a blizzard."

"It's supposed to be an easy rock-climb. We've all done more difficult things than that."

"Depends on the conditions."

"We won't be able to hang about, not with so little daylight. We'll have to get up and back fairly quickly."

"What about this – here, give me the map a minute," Jim says. "If we take the van to Altnafeadh and start from there, we could do Buachaille Etive Mor, and come back by Curved Ridge if the weather's OK . . ."

Listening, Tamsin reminds herself that the Keswick trip isn't going to be anything like as taxing – a step up from the Peak District perhaps, but nowhere near as bleak and exposed as the Scottish mountains in mid-winter. Jim loves the Gaelic names, pronouncing them with relish, as if the names have the same magnetic tug as the peaks themselves. Seeing her, he reaches out a hand and pulls her towards him. "Come and look at this, Tamsin. Doesn't it make you want to get your boots on?"

"This very minute," she says, laughing.

"Don't, Tamsin," Whistler warns. "He'll have you wading through icy torrents and bivouacking in a hut that reeks of sheep-dung."

"Hacking a cave out of the ice and eating frozen ginger-cake for breakfast," Glyn says, grinning.

"Don't believe a word," Jim says. "It's all stories we put about to make ourselves sound macho." He is still looking at the map. "I wouldn't mind doing Ben Nevis if we've got time. I've only been up the tourist route before."

"Could do," Glyn agrees. "Fort William wouldn't be a bad place to spend a couple of nights. Carn Mor Dearg is the classic winter route. You follow the arrête round to Ben Nevis . . ."

Tamsin thinks of items she has heard on the radio news: *Mountain rescue teams are searching for two climbers reported missing in Glencoe . . . A climber has fallen to his death while attempting to reach the summit of Ben Nevis . . . A mountain walker has had a lucky escape after surviving overnight in a snow-hole . . .* Jim and the others know what they're doing, she reminds herself.

They're experienced, they don't take unnecessary risks. But the element of danger is a large part of the attraction, she knows; that's why they do it in winter, when mountain conditions are at their most savage. Jim has told her about an occasion when he and Glyn came the wrong way off the summit of Moel Siabhod in a blizzard; he isn't infallible. And presumably those other climbers, the dead ones, thought they knew what they were doing too – Oh, *stop* it, she scolds herself. Why do I have to worry about everything? Why can't I just laugh, and take everything as it comes, like Josie? I shall stop worrying.

"What's this, a summit meeting?" Scott comes over and nudges Jim with his foot. "You're not being very sociable."

"OK, I'll do the genial host bit," Jim says, getting to his feet. He fills Tamsin's glass for her and then wanders round with a bottle in each hand, while Tamsin and Glyn laugh at Whistler's account of Scott's birthday last year.

"He decides to cook us a gourmet dinner. His culinary achievements up till then amount to baked beans and boiled eggs, with not altogether consistent results, but that doesn't put him off. So he gets a book from the library, makes a list, goes out foraging and comes back loaded with carrier bags. Then he shoos us all out of the kitchen, insisting that he needs privacy for his creative genius to flourish, barricades himself in and spends all day in there chopping things up and burning things. Well, when Scott does something, he doesn't do it by halves. He sets the table with candles and flowers – yes, *flowers* – and arranges us round this tiny gate-legged table, the one over there, while he bustles in and out of the kitchen attending to his masterpiece. There's me and Fiona, Jim and C – er, someone he was going out with at the time . . ."

"Candida," Tamsin supplies helpfully.

"Er, yes, Candida, and then there's Louise. All jammed together, trying not to knock over the candles and flowers every time we reach for our drinks. Scott brings the first course in. Frozen prawns, still a bit frozen, but we're all too polite to mention it. Then it's his *pièce de résistance* – Boeuf Bourguignon, or so he said. He plonks it on the middle of the table in this damned great saucepan – we haven't got casserole dishes or any refinements like that – and doles it out. We start eating, ready to compliment him on his gastronomic feat. And then gradually we start looking at each other wondering if anyone's going to say anything. We're all overcome, passing out with the fumes of our own breath. Louise says very nicely, Scott, how many garlic cloves did you put in this? And Scott says Four, that's what it said in the recipe. *Four* cloves, Louise says, no, it must be more than that, it blows your head off, it tastes more like four whole bulbs. What do you mean, Scott says, all innocence, what's bulbs? So Louise explains the difference, and he says, Well, that's what I put in then. Four bulbs. I thought that was what it meant."

"Oh, Scott's famous gourmet night." Jim comes back in time to hear the end of the story. "I remember sucking extra-strong mints for the next week and wondering whether anyone would ever sit near me in lectures again."

"We were a bit nervous in case he decided to have another go this year," Whistler says. "Fortunately he seems to have recognised his own limitations."

At about 2 a.m. the party starts to break up. People drift away in twos and threes, leaving a mess of beer cans and bottles, glasses, ashtrays, stray cassettes. Josie has gone off with someone, but Tamsin stays to help clear up.

Jim finds dustbin bags for the rubbish. "We won't bother bringing the furniture down till tomorrow. It'd make too much noise."

When the main room is more or less shipshape, Jim puts some quiet music on and goes into the kitchen to make coffee. By the time he comes back with it Scott has crashed out on one of the beds, face down, snoring softly; his coffee goes cold while the others talk. Jim sprawls on the floor beside Tamsin, leaning his head on her shoulder, and she puts her arm round his neck and his hand reaches up to clasp hers. A night-time chill is creeping through the flat but his body is close and warm. She can feel his heart beating through his shirt.

Eventually Whistler stirs. "The birthday boy's dead to the world." He gets to his feet and stretches. "Are you ready then, Fiona?" They go into his room to find their coats.

"Don't go, Tamsin," Jim whispers into her ear. "Stay with me tonight." His fingers are entwined in her hair and his breath is warm on her cheek. She closes her eyes, her pulse leaping. But there is Scott, and Whistler . . . Jim follows her train of thought, and murmurs, "Don't worry. Whistler won't come back. He'll stay at Fiona's. His room will be spare . . ."

It would be so easy to say yes – every bodily instinct is saying *yes, I want to stay*, but she doesn't. She mumbles excuses and runs away, following Whistler and Fiona downstairs into the darkness. She always seems to be running away. *No, not now, not yet.*

STRIDING EDGE

*T*he Lake District weekend offers Tamsin the chance to leave her worries behind and to give all her concentration to the physical challenge of the mountain summits. On the first day, they're going to climb Great Gable. Tamsin likes the name. It sounds impressive: not a name for a mere hill but for a real peak. She has seen pictures of its classically majestic profile; seen from the south it presents a formidable façade, a sheer precipice dropping down abruptly into the valley, fissured and scored.

"Don't worry," Jim has assured her, "we're not going up that way! It looks different from the other side. There's nothing difficult about it, just a bit of easy scrambling to get to the summit."

Tamsin hopes that easy really does mean easy. What Jim considers easy may appear very differently to her, on her first real fell walk.

Starting off from the bunkhouse on Saturday morning, it looks as if they will be disappointed in their hopes for spectacular views; it is a damp, misty day, with a heavy dew, and cobwebs clinging to the hedges. Whistler drives the minibus as far as Seatoller, a pretty village with farm cottages and a café. The walk starts by ascending the Honister Pass road as far as the Honister Hause Youth Hostel, and then they turn up a steep rocky track beside a fence, gaining height quickly towards the minor summit of Grey Knotts. Tamsin is soon hot inside her waterproofs and there is a pulse beating in her ears; every time she feels that she cannot take another step before her lungs give out, she finds that Louise has stopped too, scarlet-faced and perspiring, and they stand companionably together pretending to admire the non-existent view until they get their breath back. Andy and Jon are even slower, trailing some distance behind the main group until Whistler makes everyone wait for them. Close by, Tamsin hears the *pruk* of a raven, and sheep skitter away over the rocks on thin black legs. The mist obscures everything; there is no mountain to be seen, and she wonders whether they will ever see more than the few yards of bouldery path and stream in front of them. And then, gradually, there is a sense of sunlight not far above, filtering through the vapour, and within a few steep feet they emerge from the mist and stand in bright sunshine, exclaiming at the sudden transformation. The path above them rises clear and glistening now to the cairned summit of Grey Knotts, and they are looking down on a sea of white cloud so level that Tamsin fancies she could walk across it, or swim in it. The mist hugs the valleys, leaving the high tops clear, the slopes green-gold. Great Gable is in front of them now, its classic profile looking every bit as impressive as Tamsin has seen it in pictures; there is still a considerable distance to climb. After the exertion of the walk up, and with the damp mist gone, it is warm enough for shirt-sleeves. People start stripping off coats and sweaters and stuffing them into rucksacks, and at the cairn on Grey Knotts they stop for a coffee-break. From here, it is a short distance to the insignificant summit of Brandreth, and down into the mist again to a broad eroded track to Great Gable, where the path swoops dramatically to a narrow saddle and then rises steeply to the main summit. The scrambling requires care, but Jim is right, it is not difficult. He waits for her, and Tamsin finds herself enjoying the sensations of quickly gaining height, reaching, stretching, pausing to see the route ahead up a zigzag cairned path. She is doing it: she is climbing and is not afraid, even when she looks down to the sunlit slopes far below her feet; she feels fit and capable, following Jim's sure lead. The gradient lessens towards the mountain's bouldery summit. Jim waits for Tamsin as she mounts the last few yards, and throws his arms round her as she comes to meet him. Flushed and triumphant, she hugs him back. For him, this must be a familiar experience – the toil over, the reward earned – but he looks as exhilarated as she feels, his eyes alert with excitement.

"Great, isn't it? – this cloud inversion makes it seem like another world . . ."

"It's fantastic!"

They stand looking down over the sheer southwest face, which drops straight into lapping vapour like an incoming tide. Across the flat plain of mist, other peaks rise, blue-green, grey, inviolable, into the distance. Tamsin likes the sense that there are no valleys, no towns and road and railway lines, no ordinary life at all, only this sea of peaks floating above the everyday world. She understands now what Jim means when he says that life doesn't begin until you've climbed a mountain.

"And they're always here, these peaks and hills," she says. "Whatever we're doing all the rest of the time, sitting in lectures or having parties or asleep, they're here, above everything, like this."

It sounds stupid, but Jim laughs and says, "Yes! That's what keeps me going half the time, knowing that."

There are other parties on the summit – "There always are," Glyn says; "I bet it's hard to find standing-room up here on a fine day in summer" – and there is every encouragement to linger, bathed by the sun's weak winter warmth. Sandwiches, flasks and cameras start to appear, a leisurely lunch break follows, and it is only the threat of an early dusk that makes them get to their feet and begin the descent, reluctantly leaving the sunlit tops for the clouds and drizzle below.

Looking out of the minibus windows on the way back through Keswick, Tamsin looks pityingly at the people who have spent the day in shops and offices, not knowing how magnificent the day has been up on the heights.

The bunkhouse drying room is festooned with coats, trousers, socks, rucksacks, gaiters; getting in and out means ducking underneath damp dangling garments. The hot air smells of sweat and mud and dubbin. Jim, who is far more particular about his walking gear than he is about his everyday clothes, stays behind to wax his boots ready for tomorrow.

"I'll do yours as well if you like," he tells Tamsin.

"Thanks, but I'll do them, if you let me use your Nikwax."

"Here's a brush to get the mud off, then."

Tamsin does not want the glorious day to end. She is basking in it, her limbs tired but relaxed. She feels delirious with happiness, drunk with it, except that this is better than being drunk; a combination of high spirits, a sense of achievement, and love. In a rush of affection she links her arms round Jim's waist and kisses him. "Thank you!"

He laughs at her. "What's this for? Letting you use my boot wax?"

"For showing me Great Gable."

His arms close round her and the boot he is cleaning thuds to the floor. "And another one tomorrow – Helvellyn. I don't know why you're thanking me for it, but I'm glad you liked it today. It was a fantastic day. It still is." He kisses her, his mouth firm and eager against hers, and she responds just as keenly. Now, perversely, when there is no chance whatsoever of spending the night with Jim, no choice but to separate and go off to their single-sex dormitories, she wants to stay with him, keep hold of him, make love with him – perhaps *because* there's no chance of it. Oh, you *coward*! she mocks herself. But she doesn't feel at all cowardly now; only the sense of tingling excitement that seems to have coursed through both of them like an electrical charge. One of Tamsin's hands finds its way inside Jim's sweatshirt, exploring the length of his spine; their bodies are pressed tightly together and his mouth is against her ear, breathing quickly. The temperature in the boot room has shot up to tropical heat. And then the heady mood is spoiled when Tamsin's eyes start to itch and she blinks furiously, unable to help it.

"What's the matter?" Jim says. He leans back to look and stumbles against the dropped boot. "Something in your eye?"

"My contact lenses are steaming up in this heat."

"So are mine. And I'm not wearing any."

Tamsin laughs shakily. "Idiot!"

There is a swish of waterproof fabric as the garments hanging nearest them are pushed aside to reveal Whistler's startled face. His feet are enormous in scarlet socks and he is carrying his walking boots by the laces. Tamsin and Jim disengage themselves hastily.

"Oh, pardon me," Whistler says politely, and then grins. "I realise that opportunities for privacy are somewhat limited here, but all the same this wouldn't be my ideal choice of venue."

"I don't think you should underestimate boot rooms," Jim says. "They can be very romantic places, given the right circumstances."

By next morning the weather has taken a different turn. It feels like winter rather than balmy autumn. There is a restless, fretting wind which makes Tamsin huddle into her sweater as soon as she steps outside, and it looks like rain. Jim, Whistler and Fiona are standing outside the bunkhouse looking up at the sky.

"The forecast's not all that bad. I heard it on the local radio at seven. At least, it's not going to get much worse."

"That black cloud's moving in, though."

"The wind could get up by this afternoon."

"What d'you reckon?" Whistler asks Jim, who is to lead today's walk.

"Oh, we'll go. I can't see any reason to change

the plan. If it rains we'll get wet," Jim replies, with irrefutable logic.

In the self-catering kitchen Scott and Andy are on toast duty, wielding a blackened grill-pan and handing out browned slices as if dealing cards. Afterwards, it's Tamsin's turn to wash up, with Louise and Candida, and she is surprised to hear them discussing alternatives to the walk.

"Are you really not going?" she asks them.

"I can't see much point in slogging up Helvellyn in the rain," Candida says. "It won't be like yesterday. I've done it before, anyway."

"We were thinking of doing our own thing," Louise explains to Tamsin. "Whistler's going to drive to Patterdale, so we thought of walking round to the other side of Ullswater and perhaps getting a boat back to Glenridding. There are lots of cafés in Glenridding if it's wet. You can come with us if you like," she offers.

Tamsin hesitates, and Candida says, "Are you worried about Striding Edge? You needn't be. It's not as bad as it looks."

"I don't fancy it," Louise says, "not on a day like this, anyway."

Tamsin has already asked Jim about Striding Edge, but he said the same as Candida: not as bad as it looks. After yesterday, she feels more confident.

"No, thanks for asking, but I'll go up Helvellyn," Tamsin decides. "After all, if I don't do it today, when will I get another chance?"

By the time they reach the choppy grey expanse of Ullswater and Patterdale village at its southern end, the splinter group has swelled to five. Tamsin's optimism dwindles as she puts on her boots, realising that none of the slower walkers is left with the main party. She relies on using Louise, Andy and Jon as a measure of her own capabilities – what they can do, she can do – but the Helvellyn group setting off from Grisedale Bridge comprises only fit, tough walkers, apart from herself. Her legs are aching from yesterday's climb, although she knows that the stiffness will soon wear off. She hopes Jim won't set too fast a pace; she dreads being the one who holds up the entire party. Easygoing though Jim is in almost every other respect, he is exacting in his approach to walking expeditions, especially when he is leading and conditions are poor. People are expected to be able to look after themselves, to have adequate clothing and food, not to stray off, above all never to complain – a cheerful stoicism must be maintained under the most appalling conditions. It is the hill-walker's code, she has learned that much: what you don't like, you put up with. No one forced you to come.

Like yesterday, it is a long, steep, leg-aching climb at first, up a track to a point called The Hole in the Wall, where a stile is set into a break in the stonework. The valley to the left is lush green, sheltered and inviting in contrast to the exposed higher ground. Up here the wind is squally, lashing rain into their faces like a fine spray of gravel. Hoods are up, drawstrings tightened, and everyone ahead of Tamsin is an anonymous plodding figure on the rocky path towards the start of Striding Edge. Tamsin's foot skids on wet rock and her stomach tightens at the thought of the exposed narrow ridge ahead. She will feel much better when she is on the other side. She realises that she has underestimated the effects of bad weather on mountain terrain, even though she's heard Jim and the others discussing it often enough. The ridges and peaks which yesterday rose serene and golden above the cloud are now brooding, wind-lashed, ominous.

They are still gaining height, the higher ground opening up in front of them. Where the path winds to the right of steep crags Jim waits for everyone to catch up and shouts something which Tamsin can't hear, then leads off. She can see the switchback spine of the ridge ahead, with Jim making his way carefully but easily. Dave waits behind as the group strings out in single file, and she guesses that Jim has asked him to be back marker; you need someone experienced to bring up the rear. The wind whips her as she steps out behind Glyn on to a bare pavement of slabs worn and polished by countless boots. She tries not to panic as she realises that the rocks sheer down abruptly on each side; a few feet ahead she can descend to a lower path, with easy footholds. There are uninterrupted falls of scree either side, the bulk of Helvellyn rearing ahead. Down on the right, in an enclosed basin, is Red Tarn, not red at all but a ruffled slaty grey. On the other side, a longer drop plummets without break to the valley floor, where a stream twines like silver thread a dizzying distance below. At this altitude the rain has become hail, the wind hurling it in sharp stinging bursts, so that Tamsin pulls her hood round to protect her eyes, afraid that a contact lens may be flicked out. As the ridge narrows, the broad slabs are replaced by smaller but still reassuring footholds just below the rock crest, which humps like the armour-plated spine of a stegosaurus. Tamsin is holding Dave back, picking her way carefully, choosing handholds and footholds, not trusting herself. Ahead of her, Glyn is making far quicker progress, but she tells herself *If it's no worse than this, I can do it. Don't look down, don't look ahead. The next step is enough to think about.* But she can feel the tension rising in her throat, a panic which increases when she sees Glyn taking two steps which bring him right up to the crest of the ridge and along it for a few strides. The wind buffets her as she tries to follow. The rocks are set at awkward angles, her handholds gone unless she crouches forward, but then she feels that the wind might lift her like a sail and she will be powerless to stop herself from rolling down that terrifying drop and crashing to the rocks at the bottom. Her knees trembling, she looks for a foothold and sees the edge of her boot centimetres away from the empty fall of rain and hail and the blue-grey space yawning below. Her mind reels. It's no use giving herself calm instructions now. Fear is a clamp, gripping her, fastening her to the rock crest like a limpet. It is a primeval force, a fizzing in the pit of her stomach, a trembling which vibrates through her whole body. She cannot move a hand or a foot, cannot trust herself to move in any direction.

Behind her, Dave is waiting patiently. She is blocking the obvious route ahead. Eventually he realises she's stuck and comes up close.

"You're doing fine," he shouts encouragingly. "Go on. Bring your left foot up to that bit of a ledge there."

She looks where he is pointing. It is impossible, a stretch which is quite beyond her; what if her foot slips? Her stomach contracts with fear. If she doesn't move on in a moment and get to safety she is going to be sick.

"Glyn!" Dave bellows. The wind snatches the word away but at the same moment Glyn realises there's no one behind him and comes back to help. He moves towards her with easy assurance, as if it's no more difficult than picking his way through puddles.

"Come on, you're doing all right," he shouts to Tamsin, not knowing that she has been crouched rigid with fear for several minutes. "Put your foot here and your hand there." When he sees that she can't, or won't, he edges closer and says, "Here, give me your hand."

Tamsin tries, but that's even worse – Glyn's hand is slippery in waterproof gloves, he will pull her off-balance and she won't be able to get her feet arranged in time; she has lost all control of her limbs. She will fall and pull him off with her. "I'm sorry. I can't," she says, polite but firm. She shrinks closer to her perch, obstinate and defiant.

Dave manages to get past her by performing a balancing trick on a sloping boulder, and says to Glyn, "You wait here. I'll go and tell Jim to come back."

That's the last thing Tamsin wants to happen. She is holding up everyone now, not just Dave and Glyn but the whole group; everyone will know she has lost her nerve, and of all people she does not want Jim to realise that. But these thoughts are only ripples on the surface of her mind; deeper and far more powerful is the fear surging from underneath like a nightmare. She tries to bully herself: *Don't be stupid. If this were a six-foot wall instead of a mountain ridge, you'd walk along it without even thinking. Pretend there's no drop and you can do it*. The intuitive part of her mind refuses to listen. Her instincts are fighting with each other: *Run, run, get out of here. Don't move, stay exactly where you are or you'll fall*. Glyn keeps trying to encourage her, but she is sure he must be impatient, and getting as cold as she is. She is shivering, and the inside of her kagoule feels wet and clammy.

The green blob which is Jim is moving steadily towards her. He negotiates his way past Glyn and comes up close, his face concerned. She feels so stupid that she could cry.

"It is a bit breezy up here," he remarks conversationally.

A bit breezy – in spite of her predicament Tamsin almost laughs out loud.

"You should have taken the lower track," he says, pointing to a path she hasn't noticed a few feet lower down to her right. If she had taken it at first she might have managed, but now her mind blanks out at the thought of retracing her steps.

"I can't do it," she tells him. "It's no good. I'll have to go back."

"Don't be daft. Of course you can do it," Jim says. "You might as well go forward as back. Look, it's easy. Put your foot there and give me your right hand."

She bites her lip and tries to do what he says. At that point there is a squall of wind which bites into her face and blurs her vision, and she struggles against Jim's grasp, regaining her position.

"For God's sake, Tamsin," he shouts after three tries, "this isn't a place for dithering about. Don't look down and scare yourself. Make your mind up and do it. Can't you trust me? I won't let you fall. You've got to commit yourself."

Eventually, with Jim guiding her, she manages to go back rather than forward to a ledge three feet lower down where she has secure handholds and feels relatively safe. But she can see that Jim is getting edgy too, looking over his shoulder at the awkward places ahead if she does manage to get past this sticking-point. And then there is Swirrel Edge on the other side of the main summit. She has as much chance of negotiating it as she would a tight-rope. She realises what he is thinking, and makes up her mind.

"I'm going back," she shouts at him. "I don't want to spoil it for everyone."

"Don't be bloody stupid," he yells back. "You can't go down on your own. Everyone stays together. You'll have to have another try. We'll find a different way."

She shakes her head miserably. Nothing is going to induce her to venture on to the exposed rocks again, not even Jim's scorn if she refuses. "I can't. I'll only get stuck again, or I'll get into trouble farther along."

Jim curses, and shouts for Glyn to come over.

"It's no good. I'm going to have to take Tamsin back," he shouts. "Could you take over leading, or Dave? You've got a map and compass, haven't you? Dave knows the way."

"No! I don't want you to come back with me," Tamsin protests. "And anyway you can't. You're leading."

"There's not much choice, is there? Someone's

got to and it had better be me. You can't go wandering off on your own, that's for sure."

"I don't mind going back with Tamsin if you'd rather carry on," Glyn suggests.

"Thanks, but there's no time to have a debate about it," Jim says. "It'll be dark at this rate. I'll go. You carry on."

"OK, then," Glyn says amiably. "I'll tell the others."

Tamsin argues with Jim a bit more, but he is quite adamant: she can't go back on her own. "It's decided now, anyway. There's no point in standing here discussing it," he says shortly. "Let's get off this edge. I'll go behind to make sure you don't get stuck again."

Tamsin inches her way back, almost feeling that she would rather fall off and kill herself than face up to her failure. Her knees and hands are quivering and she feels barely in control of her limbs or her emotions. Even the broad slabs at the beginning look treacherously wet and slidy. She is trembling with cold and shock, angry with herself, angry with Jim, nearly in tears of frustration.

"What happened back there?" Jim shouts when he is able to draw level. "Did one of your contact lenses come out?"

He has presented her with the perfect excuse. All she has to say is *Yes, I lost a lens*, and neither Jim nor anyone else will think the worse of her. No one could expect her to cross an exposed ridge without being able to see properly.

"No, it wasn't that," she says. "I just got stuck, and froze up."

Already, now that the ground is firm beneath her feet instead of sheering away at both sides, she feels foolish. She has made a fuss, let herself down, she has failed. She is a liability, a nuisance, ruining the day's walk. She has committed a cardinal sin.

"It was my fault," Jim says. "I shouldn't have let you come."

Her anger at the male arrogance of that remark isn't in the least tempered by the knowledge that he does have a point. He would have done better to make up her mind for her, sending her on the easy walk; she has proved herself incapable of making her own decision and sticking to it.

"Yes, it was your fault," she yells at him. "If you're such a marvellous leader you should be able to tell people what to expect."

"I didn't know you were going to freeze up," he shouts crossly. "You should have told me you're afraid of heights. You didn't have to come. Next time –"

"You must be joking!" she flares back. "There isn't going to be a next time. Not unless I can go with a leader who knows what he's doing."

"Tamsin –"

"Oh, leave me alone!"

She turns her back on him and strides down the slope. Jim follows, not attempting to reason with her any more. They walk well apart, not even speaking. When they reach the Hole in the Wall Jim climbs the stile and waits on the sheltered side. "We'd better eat some lunch," he tells her.

She climbs the stile sulkily, avoiding looking at him. The thought of eating turns her stomach – she still feels queasy, as if sea-sick. "I don't want anything," she says, and hears her voice as petulant as a child's.

"Don't be stupid," Jim says curtly. "It's cold and it's windy and there's still a long way to go. You've got to eat." He rummages in his pack for his sandwiches and Tamsin finds hers. They eat in silence, and as soon as they set off again Jim strides ahead, so fast that she struggles to keep up. He is as remote as a stranger, a different person entirely from the one who kissed her in the boot room. It's no good trying to explain; he will never understand the terror that paralysed her. *Jim* doesn't know what it's like to freeze up with fear; he's used to treating a finger-nail's width of rock as a toehold, grappling his way up sheer cliff faces. She hasn't seen him climbing but she has seen photos of the sort of thing they do, and that alone is enough to make her stomach reel. All she wants to do is run away: far from Jim, far from the dangerous lure of the mountains. She wants to be back in her own room, out of her clammy wet gear; she wants to soak in a hot bath and forget the whole humiliating experience. But first she will have to wait with Jim while the others complete the circuit of Helvellyn, Swirrel

Edge, Red Tarn, and then she will have to face their pity, or scorn. Hot angry tears sting her eyes and she blinks them away, increasingly furious with herself, furious with Jim.

He takes her a different way back, down a steep grassy slope towards Glenridding and Ullswater, finally joining brackeny paths and then a farm lane leading to the village. Tamsin dreads bumping into Candida and Louise and having to explain why they have come back early, though everyone is sure to know sooner or later. Near the bridge there is a walkers' café, cheerfully lit. "We might as well get a hot drink while we wait," Jim says. "There's nothing else to do."

In the warm fug inside, three men sit round a table, dressed in walking gear, with stocky legs in breeches, gaiters and boots. They are laughing uproariously, in marked contrast to the irritable atmosphere Tamsin and Jim bring in with them. Whenever Jim speaks to Tamsin she snaps back at him as if it's all his fault; soon he gives up and they drink their coffee in silence. She can sense Jim's relief when one of the men turns to him with the instant camaraderie of hill-walkers and says, "Been up on top, then? Bit blowy today."

"Not right up to the summit, no," Jim replies. Not wanting to hear what else he might say, Tamsin goes outside and wanders over the road towards the edge of Ullswater. The rain has lifted, and down here there is only a light breeze; it's hard to imagine how terrifying it was on

Striding Edge, up in the wind. Glenridding is obviously a small tourist centre, with a big hotel, teashops and postcard stands, a coach parked by the lakeside. Ducks swim up hopefully when Tamsin walks to the shore; she throws them pieces of cake from her packed lunch and they scramble for it, quacking. Ducks, tourists, everyone but her are perfectly happy.

It is all over with Jim, she knows. It will never be the same again.

WOLF MAN

Catastrophic though the day has been, Tamsin feels sad to leave the Lake District behind. As if to make up for the turbulent weather earlier in the day, dusk falls in a glowing wash of colour, the peaks clear now, purple and other-worldly against a charcoal-streaked sky of soft blue, rose, gold. Tamsin gazes out of the back window of the minibus until the last glimpse of the Lakeland hills fades and the scenery becomes flattened and undramatic on each side of the motorway. She knows she will have to come back. In spite of everything, she has fallen under the spell of crag, tarn, the light shifting over high peaks.

She and Jim haven't spoken to each other since she left him in the café, although she has apologised to Glyn and Dave for being a nuisance and they both shrugged it off, saying that it didn't matter in the slightest. But then she hasn't yelled at them and called them useless or refused to speak to them civilly. To Jim and herself, it matters out of all proportion. When the minibus arrives back at the campus, Jim looks as if he might be going to say something to her, but she quickly picks up her boots and bag and marches off before he has the chance; she can't look him in the face. She is sure everyone knows how fed up they are with each other, and that makes it worse. The others are probably sympathising with him for being lumbered with her.

Not any more.

It is a relief to get back to the routines of lab-work next morning. Tamsin's group is in the metallurgy lab learning how to do tensile tests. They are clustered round a guillotine-like structure, the Instron, and their lecturer has four-inch test-pieces of various kinds of metal lined up ready; the aim is to measure the pressure at which each kind of metal will break. He demonstrates how to clamp the test-piece in position to the load cell at the bottom and the crosshead above, and then activates the hydraulics, making the crosshead exert force upwards; it is like a torture rack for metals. A pen scratches as the chart recorder linked to the machine makes a graph showing the pressure.

"You can see the test-piece thinning out now, or necking," Mike says, as the piece of steel gradually assumes the shape of an elongated hour-glass, "and –"

There is a resounding metallic bang which

makes everyone within earshot jump and clasp their hands over their ears and the floor of the lab reverberate. The steel specimen is now in two funnel-shaped pieces. Later, the students will examine the fracture surface under the scanning electron microscope. They watch while three other specimens are tested – silvery aluminium, titanium like a light stainless steel, dark bluish nickel alloy. For each, they record the load at which it fails. Less impressive than steel, nickel alloy breaks with a feeble snap. The students are not allowed to use the Instron machine because it is too susceptible to damage, but later in the session they pair off to use the simpler Houndsfield machine, a table-top alternative which is manually operated.

Tamsin tries to forget her own weaknesses in examining those of metals. The laboratory is a safe zone. You follow the procedures and the materials behave as they should; everything is predictable, known, charted.

"How was your weekend?" Rikayah asks over lunch.

"Good and bad," Tamsin says, not wanting to elaborate.

"What, the weather?"

"Yes, partly. What about yours? How were your family?"

Rikayah smiles, and says, "Fine. We're all looking forward to my cousin's wedding in the spring. It will be a very big family occasion – all my aunts and uncles are coming over from Kenya."

"Who's she marrying?" Tamsin asks.

"Someone her parents chose," Rikayah says.

Tamsin tries not to look too astonished. Rikayah continues, "I've seen him a few times at parties and he seems very suitable. My cousin has been allowed to meet him and get to know him a little – her parents aren't as strict as some. In a really strict arranged marriage the girl wouldn't be allowed to meet her husband until the wedding."

"What about you?" Tamsin asks. "You won't have an arranged marriage, will you?" It doesn't seem compatible with being at university and preparing for a career in Engineering. All the same, she has seen for herself that Rikayah's way of life embraces two cultures.

"Many Asian girls do choose for themselves these days," Rikayah says, "but as I told you we're quite traditional in my family. I don't think my parents will actually choose for me but I'd certainly want to marry someone they approved of. We don't really go out with people, the way Western couples do."

"But what would happen if you wanted to marry someone who isn't a Muslim?"

"I suppose that's possible," Rikayah says, "but it would make things very difficult. I would certainly want my parents to be involved at an early stage." She looks at Tamsin for a reaction and adds, "I know many people find the whole business very strange, but in our culture we think marriage is too important to be left to chance. You only have to look at the rate of failure when people choose for themselves."

"Yes," says Tamsin, for whom this is rather a sore point just now.

There are only three weeks until the end of term. Tamsin wants them to go quickly. The course itself is going well, but everything else seems to be turning out disastrously – her meeting with her father, her attempt at mountain walking, the rift with Jim. She needs to recover, to put time and distance between herself and these traumas.

On Friday, she finds an E-mail message from Jim: **All right, Sunday was a write-off, but it's not the end of the world. How about a drink at Rafferty's tonight?**

She sends back: **Sorry, but I've got too much work to do.**

It is a brush-off, and Jim will know it is: no one in their first year has such a heavy workload that they can't take a Friday night off, unless they're exceptionally devoted. She isn't sure why, when Jim is clearly willing to make up their quarrel, she isn't eager to pick up the relationship again. Perhaps it is just as well if she doesn't see him any more, she rationalises; Sunday's events were as good a way as any of letting her know that it wasn't going to work. The extent of her involvement had begun to frighten her: it was happening so fast and so wonderfully that she had been waiting for something to go wrong. He would turn out like her father after all, or he would get bored with her, or something awful would happen on one of his climbing trips; it hadn't occurred to her that she might deliberately drive him away. Now that it's over, it seems inevitable that it was short-lived. She will have to forget about it. She reminds herself that she is here to do a degree, not to agonise over a failed relationship. She will be more careful from now on. Temporary madness, her mother described it, and from Tamsin's newly disillusioned position that seems a fairly accurate description. Fortunately it *was* only temporary.

None of her reasoning helps her to feel any calmer when she sees Jim by chance on Friday night. She goes to see *The Royal Hunt of the Sun* with Rikayah and Tatsuya, and Jim is there in the audience with Fiona and Whistler. He sees her come in and she flushes guiltily, thinking of her electronic lie.

"There's Jim over there," Rikayah says a few moments later. "Don't you want to sit with him?"

"Oh – that's all off now," Tamsin says awkwardly.

At the end of the play Jim gets up and leaves without a word or glance. Tamsin tries to tell herself that this was what she wanted, and hides her misery by waiting behind with the others to see Josie, who is celebrating wildly with the rest of the cast, euphoric with success.

Striding Edge was not Tamsin's first failed ascent.

She can remember a holiday with her mother at the seaside in Devon, years ago, just the two of them. Sometimes Mum took her to the fair or the swimming-pool on the sea-front, and often they went down to the beach, spending all day there with a picnic. One day they went to a different beach, away from the town, which meant going across the river on a ferry boat and then walking quite a long way along a grassy cliff path. Mum had brought one bag with their picnic food in it and another full of her painting things; Tamsin had a bucket and spade and a book. They paddled in the rock pools for a while looking for crabs and shrimps, and then after their picnic Mum got out her sketch-pad and her tubes of water-colour paint. Tamsin knew that she was expected to play by herself now.

They were a long way from the main beach where there were deckchairs and an ice-cream van and sometimes donkeys. There was no one else here at all. Tamsin spent a long time sorting stones into groups of different colours and then she started to feel bored. She had finished her book and there was no one to play with.

She wandered along the shingle looking up at the cliff. It was bouldery, with gorse bushes and tufty grass springing up in the spaces between rocks. A zigzag path came down to it, the path they had climbed down very carefully to get to the beach, but farther along there was no path, just rocks and grass going straight up, higher than Tamsin could see. There were ledges up there where Mum said birds would nest: fulmars, she said, those birds that look like gulls but fly with stiff wings like balsa-wood aircraft models.

Tamsin looked along the beach to where Mum sat sketching some rocks. She decided to give Mum a surprise by climbing all the way up past the birds' nests and then walking along the cliff path to shout at her from above.

She chose her spot carefully and began to climb, giggling to herself as she imagined Mum's surprised face when she saw how high she was. The climbing was easy, new footholds and handholds appearing as she hoisted herself up. At first she enjoyed the mild thrill of frightening herself by looking down to see how far she had climbed. Then, gradually, the route ahead became less clear; she stretched a leg to reach a foothold and dry earth crumbled away, her foot dangling into space. Her heart pounded and her hands scrabbled wildly, clinging to dried twigs and stalks, as her right foot came to rest perilously beside her left. She dared not look down, and the rocks above offered nothing more substantial than crumbly clods and pink tufty flowers. She was stuck.

"Mummy!" Her voice was a thin wail. She had chosen her spot too well; Mum was out of sight round a shoulder of cliff. Her hands were weakening, her fingers losing their grip. The top of the cliff, the smooth grass slope, was not far above her now, she could see the gradient easing, a curve of path in a dip, but the distance between stretched out like elastic. Below her, the tide was coming in, its powerful blue-green surge washing over flat rocks and then fizzing into foam, sucking back. Her head swam. She started to cry, the tears trickling down her cheeks and into her mouth. And then there was someone above her, a man, leaning down.

"All right, sweetheart. Hang on there. I've got you."

He was huge, filling the whole sky as he leaned. An arm reached down, with a big brown hand at the end of it. Tamsin shrank back, terrified. What had Mum always told her? *You must never, never go off with strange men. Whatever they tell you, you must always say no.* She was caught now between two horrors. Either she would fall down the cliff, tumbling and bouncing like a stone to crash on the rocks at the bottom, or the strange man would get her and do whatever strange men do.

"No!" she screamed.

The man retreated out of sight and she thought she had scared him away. But he was only altering his position to try again. He knelt sideways and lowered a foot in a huge black boot towards her face. He was going to try to kick her off.

"Don't move now," he warned. "Stay right where you are." He spoke in a funny way, rolling his words in his mouth.

"Mum!" she shouted again. Her voice was high and frightened, floating into the gaps between the rocks, powerless to reach her mother. The man would push her off and pretend it was an accident.

"All right, sweetheart. We'll soon have you back with your mum." He had come to one side of her and a little below, legs braced, one hand grasping a secure projection of rock above. The big voice was close now; a strong arm swooped round her waist and she was lifted off her feet. Her cry of fear was choked to silence as she felt herself hoisted the last few yards, over the ragged edge where the cliff had slipped away from the grass at the top. She pitched forward on to her knees and then scrambled to her feet, away from the edge. The ground was wonderfully firm, bearing her up; she had never appreciated ground so much before. But the man was still there, levering himself up, holding her arm tightly. He stood upright and was even bigger than she thought, a huge bulk of a man, strong, hairy. She knew she must run away before he did what strange men did next – offered her sweets and tried to entice her into his car. A sob rose in her throat. She had escaped from the cliff but now she was even farther from Mum. She would never see her again.

The man took out a handkerchief that looked as big as a table-cloth, pulling yards of it out of his pocket, and wiped her eyes and face with it.

"Gave yourself a nasty fright, didn't you?" he said in his rolling voice. He smiled at her. His teeth were big, like everything else about him, with gaps between. Big Bad Wolf teeth. She pulled back but his grip was firm. He wouldn't let go of her now that he had her.

"Let's find your mummy then, shall we? Where is she?"

"Down there. On the beach." Tamsin pointed, realising too late that he had tricked her. The beach was lonely, deserted. The Wolf Man would take her down to Mum and then he would have both of them.

He picked up a khaki rucksack from the grass and slung it over one shoulder. Tamsin started to sob uncontrollably, submitting as the man took her hand in his and led her carefully down the path. His hand was so big that he could crush the bones in her fingers if he wanted to.

"There, there, sweetheart," he kept saying. "It's all over now. We'll soon have you back with your mummy."

They heard her before they saw her. She was shouting, "Tamsin! Tamsie! Where are you?" in a voice high and tight with fear. Slithering down the last few yards, Tamsin saw the painting things abandoned near the rocks, tubes of paint scattered, a plastic water-cup bobbing on the tide. Mum was running along the beach in little frantic rushes, staring wildly at the dark gaps in the rocks.

"Over here!" the Wolf Man shouted.

Mum did not so much turn as fling her body round to face them. She rushed up to them, her sandalled feet skidding on the stones, her eyes wide with fright as she saw Tamsin and the Wolf Man. She snatched Tamsin back, hugging her until neither of them could breathe.

"Better keep a closer eye on her next time," the Wolf Man said.

He started explaining what had happened. Mum thanked him, and thanked him again and again, and he went away, climbing up the zigzag. He wasn't a monster after all, just an ordinary man who had come to help.

"Oh, *Tamsie*," Mum said. Tamsin couldn't tell whether she was pleased or cross, or who she was cross with. Mum's eyes were wet and shiny, her mouth tight as if she would let too much out if she opened it. And then she started to sob, holding her hand over her mouth as if trying to hold it all in. Her shoulders shook and she made funny gulping noises, and then she knelt down to collect the picnic things together as if nothing was happening, but Tamsin could tell she was crying. Tamsin tried to help, pushing things into the basket, finding a knife half-buried in the sand.

"I'm a hopeless mother," Mum managed to say, mopping at her eyes with a tissue.

"No!" Tamsin said in a small voice. She didn't know what was happening. She had never seen her mother cry before and it frightened her more than being stuck on the cliff, more than the Wolf Man, more than anything.

Tamsin comes back from a late-afternoon lecture to find Josie in hushed conference outside the open door of Julia's room with Liz, Julia's friend. The room has been cleared. The shelves are bare, the bed stripped, the sheets crumpled on the floor. Even Julia's name-tag is missing from the door.

"What's happened?" Tamsin asks. "Where's Julia?"

Josie pulls a wry face. "She's gone."

"She's packed in her course," Liz says. "Gone home."

Tamsin stares. "Why? Did she think she wouldn't pass?"

"The course was fine," Liz says. "It was Steve. He's finished with her, told her it's all over for good. We tried to talk her out of going but she wouldn't listen. Packed all her bags and got her sister to come and collect her."

Tamsin is appalled. It's no fun ending a relationship, she knows that much, but even so . . . "She's given her course up just because of some *man*?" She has never worked out who Julia's man is, although it's abundantly clear that he wields undue influence over her. "Who is this Steve anyway? Why does she let him tread all over her?"

"Didn't you know?" Liz says. "It's Steve Balderson, *Dr* Balderson. Her course tutor. He'd have been grading her special assignment, setting the final exams, writing her references . . . everything."

Tamsin lets this sink in. She understands now why the mystery man has never called round for coffee or dropped in like most people's boyfriends. It must have been a situation fraught with difficulty.

"It's been on and off for months," Liz says, "and if she'd had any sense she would have told him where to get off a long time ago. Everyone could see she was heading for a big disappointment, except Julia. Now his wife's found out about it and he's panicked."

The urge to escape from unbearable situations is familiar enough for Tamsin to feel sympathy for Julia. "All the same, to throw away her chance of a degree! Couldn't she have asked for a different tutor? Though I suppose it would be serious for him if anyone knew the reason."

"I don't think she was in a state to be that logical about it," Josie says. "Either that or she didn't want to land him in trouble. Though God knows why she should care."

Liz kicks at the skirting board with her toe.

"He'll be all right," she says savagely. "Men like that always are. I suppose he'll wait till the dust settles at home and then start stringing along the best-looking girl from his next group."

A large soft parcel arrives for Tamsin. She opens it to find a silky garment in green peacocky colours, and a note from Aunt Rachel: *Mum said you didn't have anything to wear for the Christmas dance , so I thought this might do if you don't think it looks too dated. It's loose enough for the fit not to matter much. If you've already got something else, don't worry – bring it home at Christmas. I hope you have as good a time wearing it as I did at the Oxford May Ball.*

Tamsin has forgotten about the dance. She holds up the dress and then looks at her reflection in the washbasin mirror. It is full-length, a twenties style, simply cut and falling straight from a scooped neck. The colours are beautiful: deep blues and sea-greens, glowing against each other. Aunt Rachel's hair is greying a little now but it was once the same auburn as Tamsin's, and she must have known that the colours of the dress would suit Tamsin as well as they had once suited her.

Tamsin sends a card in reply: *Thanks, fairy godmother. It's perfect.*

The only problem is that she has no interest at all in going to the dance. Next day, though, Tatsuya repeats his invitation and this time she accepts. Tatsuya is just a friend and she needs to cheer herself up; Jim won't be there, so she needn't worry about bumping into him.

She makes an effort to feel Christmassy. She goes out carol singing with the Animal Rights group to raise money for the Anti-Live Export Campaign, and goes shopping in town for Christmas cards and presents. Writing her cards that evening, she hesitates over whether or not to send one to Jim, eventually choosing a humorous cartoon picture of reindeer and writing in it *Best wishes for a happy Christmas and good climbing in Scotland, Tamsin*. It is so bland and impersonal that she wonders if there is any point in sending it, but she still puts it on the pile with the others. After all, she is going to see Jim next term with the walking group – she doesn't intend to give that up, in spite of making a fool of herself – and they might as well be friendly towards each other. It will be easier next term, she hopes.

There is an air of great excitement on Saturday evening as people get ready for the dance, dashing in and out of each other's rooms, borrowing make-up, asking for advice on shoes or jewellery. Tatsuya comes up to call for Tamsin, very formally, looking glossy and exotic in a dinner jacket. The main hall has been transformed for the occasion, with a towering Christmas tree, glittering decorations, tables spread with food, and a vast net of silver balloons suspended from the ceiling. Self-conscious in her dress, Tamsin is not sure how to behave; everyone is so unrecognisably glamorous that it feels like being transported to Hollywood.

"Hello," says someone in ruby-red taffeta with hair piled up. "Like the dress. I'm going to be your neighbour next term, did you know?"

It's Louise. Tamsin blinks, adjusts, and says, "You're having Julia's room?"

"Yes. Lucky for me. The flat I'm in is primitive at the best of times and bloody freezing in winter. When water started coming down the walls I reported it to the Accommodation Officer and they're moving me into hall."

Tamsin is cheered by the news. She likes Louise. It will be fun having her two doors away.

"Who did you come with in the end?" she asks.

Louise looks embarrassed. "Er . . . with Jim. He wasn't going to come but I dragged him along."

Tamsin follows Louise's gaze to where Jim is standing by the Christmas tree, talking to Whistler and Fiona. He is far smarter than she has ever seen him, and his long and still rather untidy hair gives him an artistic look, like a concert pianist. She wrenches her gaze away from him.

"I thought he didn't have a smart suit?" she says. "He said he hates dressing up like a penguin."

"They've got one between them that belongs to the flat," Louise says. "Left behind by a previous occupant. Jim's the only one it fits – Whistler's too tall and Scott's too wide. It's a bit moth-eaten if you look at it closely but it's still a lot smarter than anything Jim's got."

Tamsin doesn't expect to have the chance to look at it closely. She risks another glance at Jim and at the same moment he looks across at her; she smiles uncertainly but Jim looks away without responding. Ridiculously deflated by this – well, what did you *expect*, she wonders – she realises that Tatsuya is standing by her side, virtually ignored, and introduces him to Louise. People are starting to dance, and Louise says, "Well, I'd better get back. Jim will think I've abandoned him."

Tatsuya asks Tamsin to dance, very politely, as if it is an enormous privilege; he has beautiful manners, and he is a good dancer too. Candida is dancing with someone Tamsin doesn't recognise (Toby seems to have had his day); she is fashionably understated in slinky black, with her blonde hair caught up high and tumbling over one bare shoulder. Tamsin is guiltily aware that she ought to be giving more attention to Tatsuya – it's not his fault she's preoccupied – but nevertheless finds herself thinking about Jim and Candida. Presumably Candida used to stay the night at Jim's flat; she certainly isn't prissy or prudish. Tamsin hates to think of them together, laughing, kissing, their hands roving over each other's bodies. Candida wouldn't have run away like a frightened schoolgirl. Candida wouldn't have lost her nerve on Striding Edge; she would have skipped across with the others and said it was nothing compared to the Matterhorn – Oh, *stop* it! Tamsin tells herself angrily; what does it matter now? It can't make any difference to me. And for the rest of the evening she chats to Tatsuya and Rikayah and Ken, and laughs, and dances, and watches Jim partnering Louise, and tells herself that she doesn't mind at all.

CHRISTMAS

"*I* do wish," Abigail says in a carefully neutral voice, "you'd told me you were going to track down your father. It was a bit of a shock, finding out about it from him."

"Oh, God," Tamsin mutters.

Her mother looks at her in reproach. "I know you're an adult now and you're entitled to make contact with him if you want to, but I would have liked to *know*."

"I was going to tell you," Tamsin says guiltily. "Tonight. I didn't know how to start. I didn't think he'd be so daft as to actually contact you."

"Well, he did."

"When?"

"Couple of weeks ago. He phoned." Tamsin's mother squirts washing-up liquid into the bowl viciously, as if she'd prefer to squirt it in Paul Strivener's eye. It is Tamsin's first evening at home and they are clearing up after supper.

"I didn't give him your number!" Tamsin defends herself. "How did he get it?"

"He rang Mum first. That wasn't difficult, because she's in the directory. He made up some tale about wanting to buy a painting of mine and she gave him the number." She glances at Tamsin suspiciously. "You must have told him that much. About the painting."

"Yes, I did," Tamsin admits. "Well, he needed to know. That you're a success at it. *He* never was." I gave him all the information he needed, she thinks: it's my fault. I should have warned Mum. "I'm sorry," she says inadequately. "What did he say?"

Her mother still looks a bit too deliberately under control. She doesn't actually ask *what did you think of him*? but Tamsin guesses that she must be bursting to know. "Oh, that he met you," Abigail says, rattling knives and forks into the bowl, "and that you got on so well together, and he was really looking forward to seeing you again –"

"He told you *what*? We got on well together? Oh Mum, that's not true!" Tamsin understands why her mother feels betrayed. "It was nothing like that! I did go to look for him, yes, I wanted to know what he's like, but as for seeing him again –"

She explains what happened: about turning up unexpectedly at Luxury Floorings, her impression of Paul, the meal, her hasty exit. Abigail listens without comment, washing up steadily, then unclamps enough to say, "I haven't been fair to you, really. I shouldn't have made it a taboo subject. It's natural for you to be curious about him."

"But I should have told you. Just in case he did something daft."

Abigail gives a shaky smile. "At least now it's out in the open. It was a shock and a half when I heard his voice – like a ghost popping up from the past."

"What did he talk about?"

"Oh, lots of things. Most of them stupid. I was so shocked to hear his voice, out of the blue, that I just stood there mesmerised and listened to it all."

"But *what*?" Tamsin persists, not at all sure that she wants to know.

"Oh, he was – trying to smarm round me, I suppose. God knows what he thought he was doing. I suppose he must have changed a lot – well, that's inevitable, after more than eighteen years. But I could *hear* that smile, over the phone – that charming smile of his that used to be irresistible. As if he thought he could get round me even now – you're dripping water all over the floor." She takes the saucepan Tamsin is holding and puts it back on the draining board.

"Get round you for what?" Tamsin says, although she can guess.

Abigail gives a contemptuous humph. "You

wouldn't believe it. He wanted us to meet up, me and him – go out for a meal together or something. He started by telling me about your meeting, made it sound as if the two of you were teaming up behind my back. I couldn't believe the cheek of the man! He even had the nerve to say he *regretted* what he did – as if you can walk out on someone and then turn up eighteen years later and say Sorry and expect it to be forgotten!" She looks at Tamsin sharply. "He always was a liar. I should have remembered that."

"Didn't you believe anything he said?" Tamsin asks carefully.

Abigail finishes scrubbing the grill-pan, then tips the water out of the bowl before answering.

"I don't know. I mean, that humble act – I don't think it was *all* put on. Otherwise why phone at all? But I certainly wouldn't *trust* him. Perhaps I shouldn't say that sort of thing to you any more," Abigail says doubtfully, "not now that you've contacted him. I mean, he's your father now, isn't he? He's real, not just a name you've heard mentioned."

Tamsin finishes drying the knives and forks in silence and then says, "I suppose he told you he's married?"

"Oh yes, he did mention it in passing, as though it was a minor inconvenience. And did he tell you he wished he had children of his own?" Abigail tosses her hair back as she takes off her apron and hangs it up. "No wonder he was pleased when you appeared from nowhere. Now he thinks he's got rights over you, and he can stroll along and claim his share."

"It's not me he wants," Tamsin says uneasily; "it's you."

"I don't know about that. Perhaps he thinks he can get two for the price of one. Well, he's not going to get round me that easily, even if you . . . well . . ." Abigail pauses, one hand on the kettle, and then speaks with her face turned away. "If you want to keep in touch with him, I won't interfere. I mean it. It's your right, and you're an adult now. That's what I told him."

"Mum! I –" Tamsin begins to protest, but she isn't at all sure what she wants to say. Her mother's defiance has gone; there is resignation in the droop of her shoulders and the set of her mouth as she fills the kettle and clatters its lid back in place. Tamsin wants to hug her, but Paul Strivener is invisibly between them, intruding. Mentally, she shoves him out of the way and takes the kettle. "Here, let me make the coffee. I don't want to see him again, honestly, Mum! I told him that."

Christmas dinner is at Nan's house, with Aunt Rachel and Uncle Don and their two children, Rosie and Mark. It is three months since Tamsin last saw Nan; she looks older than Tamsin remembers, small, a little greyer, rather frail. She will be seventy next year. But seventy isn't *old*,

Tamsin reassures herself; lots of people are fit and active at seventy, playing sports, taking up new interests, climbing mountains. And Nan is active around the house and garden, cooking, decorating, visiting friends and going to meetings. It is when she sits between her two daughters, Rachel and Abigail, that she looks shrunken and faded. Tamsin notices that both of them are concerned, attentive. "No, don't get up, Mum – you stay there." "I'll make the brandy sauce, don't worry."

"Is Nan all right?" Tamsin asks Abigail when they go into the kitchen to check the Christmas pudding.

Abigail hesitates, pushing a fork into the pudding and releasing a delicious smell of brandy and hot spices.

"She's been a bit poorly, on and off. I've tried to get her to come and stay with me, but she won't. I've been coming round most days after work, and Rachel's been coming over when she can."

"What does the doctor say?"

"She doesn't really know, but they're trying a course of antibiotics. You know Mum – she doesn't fuss, but she's always so active that you can easily tell when she's under the weather."

Under the weather, poorly. Mum doesn't usually talk like that: she sounds like a nurse at an old people's home. In a minute she'll say *Of course Nan's marvellous for her age* or *Creaking gates last longest.* Tamsin feels sure that the euphemisms conceal a hopeless situation.

Abigail puts the pudding on a plate, decorates it with holly and then carries it in, with a box of matches ready. Suddenly Nan looks fifty years younger, clapping her hands, exclaiming with the children as Abigail sets fire to the pudding and flames leap round it like a fiery blue halo. Abigail serves it out and everyone searches for the old-fashioned sixpences which Nan puts in the pudding each year. It is one of the family traditions, safe, reassuring: except that it used to be Grandad Charlie who lit the pudding and carried it in and served it, always contriving to get the sixpences in the children's portions. Nan's eyes are bright with pleasure at seeing the whole family present, complete. Minus one for Grandad, plus one for Aunt Rachel's three-year-old son, like figures on a balance sheet.

They exchange presents after lunch. Nan gives Tamsin a year's membership of the Youth Hostel Association, and Abigail's present to her is a new rucksack, a smart one with zipped side pockets and clipper fastenings that will be quick to undo with cold numbed hands, easier than the rusted buckles on Tamsin's tatty old one. They are so keen to encourage her that she decides not to mention her recent disgrace.

Tamsin gives her grandmother a book, *The People's War*.

"Did Abby tell you I'm helping someone who's writing a book about the war?" Nan says, leafing through it.

"No, I forgot."

"What sort of book?" Tamsin asks.

"A book about the RAF in wartime," Nan explains. "Not a history, more of a – what would you call it? – a social documentary, I suppose. Something like this one, only completely based on ordinary people's memories – people who were in the air force doing various kinds of jobs. The chap writing it wants to meet as many ex-RAF people as he can."

"Who is he?" Aunt Rachel asks. "Anyone we'll have heard of?"

"I don't think so. This is his first book – he's a freelance journalist, and his own father was in Bomber Command; that's why he's interested. Someone had passed on Charlie's name and address, not knowing that Charlie had died, but when I told this chap Roger that I was in the WAAF he wanted to come round and talk to me. We had quite a long chat, and he's coming back again after Christmas when I've sorted out my old photos and letters. It's odd," she remarks, gazing at the children who are playing in front of the fire with their new puzzles, "how clear it all is. It could have been yesterday."

Tamsin remembers the conversation with Grandad, the photographs of dead faces.

"Could I see your photos and things as well, Nan, when you get them out?" she asks. "I'd like to."

Nan looks pleased. "Of course you can, love.

Come round one day and we'll have a good old reminisce."

On the evening of Boxing Day Tamsin and Abigail watch two films in succession, share a bottle and a half of wine, eat too many chocolates and get rather light-headed. Paul Strivener hasn't been mentioned since Tamsin's first evening at home and she senses that both of them regard him as a subject best left alone for the time being. But Tamsin hasn't forgotten that there might be other men in her mother's life now.

"You haven't told me about the box numbers yet," Tamsin reminds her. "What's been happening? Where are all these men? I thought there'd be two or three turning up every day."

Abigail laughs. She is sitting cross-legged on the sofa wearing leggings and a loose printed shirt, her hair untidy. She looks twenty-five at the most. It occurs to Tamsin that there is only twelve years' difference in age between her mother and Whistler.

"It's interesting, I can say that much," Abigail says. "Very hit and miss. There was one man who sounded quite pleasant on the phone, but voices can be misleading – when he turned up he looked at least fifteen years older than he claimed to be, and he spent the whole evening telling me the faults of all the women he'd ever known. I didn't give him the chance to find out mine. Then there was one who had a whole list of questions as if I was being interviewed for a job. At some point I obviously failed, much to my relief."

"There was one you said was worth seeing again," Tamsin recalls. "What's happened to him?"

"Henry? Yes, he's all right. Interesting, funny, good company. Which is quite rare, as I'm fast finding out. I'll probably see him again after Christmas."

"Why don't you invite him round for a meal or something while I'm at home?" Tamsin suggests. For some reason she feels well-disposed towards Henry, as if any other man would be preferable to Paul Strivener.

Abigail smiles mischievously. "So that you can give him the once-over? Definitely not. I'm not having my daughter vet my men friends for me."

"I wouldn't. I don't think I'm very well qualified to offer advice," Tamsin says, only half joking.

"That wasn't what you said before you left. You seemed ready enough to supervise the proceedings then. Anyway, it hasn't reached the stage of having him round to meet the family." Abigail leans back and gazes at the Christmas cards strung round the fireplace. "Isn't it ridiculous? Even now I keep thinking, at the back of my mind, that some wonderful man is going to turn up and make my life complete. At my age I ought to know better. There's no such person."

"No," Tamsin says sadly.

Abigail looks at her. "That sounded heartfelt. What about you? You haven't said anything to me, but Mum said you mentioned someone you liked. Something to do with the mountain walking, I gathered?"

"Yes. But it didn't work out." Tamsin doesn't want to say any more about it; Jim didn't even send her a Christmas card. "We're all right though, aren't we, the two of us? We can manage without men."

"Course we can. Better off without them." Abigail uncurls herself, stands up and stretches. "I'm going to make some coffee. I need to sober up before I go to bed."

Working in the local supermarket, Tamsin has never known the time pass so slowly. Dressed in a cap and overall she sits at a checkout watching groceries slide towards her. She picks them up in rhythmic movements, pasta shells, Kit-E-Kat, bran flakes, scanning bar-codes until her head feels like bleeping in response. She goes round to see Becky and Greg, meets Rikayah at the Tate Gallery, and reads *The Return of the Native*. A deep male voice which identifies itself as Henry telephones for her mother; Tamsin is intrigued, but Henry does not appear in person.

Listening idly to the radio news over New Year, she clicks into alertness when she hears *Two climbers have been found dead in the Cairngorms*. She didn't think Jim and the others were going to the Cairngorms, but nevertheless she makes a point of listening to the later bulletin and is guiltily relieved to hear that the dead climbers were husband and wife.

Nan has been sorting out her scrapbooks and albums.

"This is my friend Felicity." She shows Tamsin a photograph of a smiling blonde girl with waved hair and pencilled eyebrows. "I met her on the first day of training and we've kept in touch ever since. She was quite a stunner, as you can see. She had dozens of boyfriends when we were together at Windersby. Even officers, and we weren't allowed to go out with officers."

"Did you ever have an officer boyfriend, Nan?"

"Not really. There was one, but he was only a friend." Nan turns the page and points. "This chap here. But I never did go out with lots of men, like Felicity. I was too keen on one special person to bother with anyone else."

"I know. Grandad told me once. He showed me the photo."

"Did he? Yes, Charlie knew him as well, of course." Nan turns the pages and stops at the photograph Tamsin has seen before. "Here he is. David."

Tamsin looks closely. This time, the first thing she notices is how young he is – hardly older than herself. Wartime aircrew aren't the big capable men she once imagined, but just like people she knows at university, hardly older than she is. "He's good-looking, isn't he?" she says.

"Oh yes, he was. Such a waste . . . all of them. He went missing more than fifty years ago, on a raid to Berlin. I never knew what happened to him; no one did. It was so awful for his parents as well as for me. He was their only son – they had no other children. He was only twenty-one."

Jim's age.

"Grandad told me about it," Tamsin says. She tries to imagine the extraordinary tensions of Nan's romance. "What was it like, Nan, knowing someone who was – well, who was practically bound to get killed, according to what Grandad said?"

"Well, it was the same for everyone," Nan says, "although whether that made it better or worse, I'm not sure. Everyone knew the risks. There would always be losses, but it was particularly bad around that time. People didn't talk about it much – it was a way of pretending it wasn't happening. David used to tell me about the flying at first, but after a while he stopped – I don't think he could talk about it. But I used to imagine it for myself every time he flew. Cramped into that Lancaster in the darkness – the cockpit was very small, I've been in one. The flak would be soaring up, the searchlight cones waiting to pin you, and for all you knew there was a German fighter sitting right underneath you with guns aimed. There was only a tiny escape hatch to get out through if you were hit, the plane might be on fire or going down in a spin, but somehow you'd try to get out. And then you'd leap out over enemy territory in the dark and hope your parachute opened . . ."

The description is enough to make Tamsin's stomach lurch with fear.

"How did ordinary people do it without going mad?" she says.

"I don't know," Nan says simply. She looks at the photograph for a few moments and then says, "I don't suppose Charlie told you about the row we'd had?"

"You and Grandad?" Tamsin says, imagining jealousy.

"No. Me and David. We'd had a stupid argument that last afternoon before he flew off to Berlin. I've never forgiven myself for it."

"What did you argue about?"

"Well . . . he wanted us to get married, and I didn't think we should rush into it so soon. Of course we wouldn't have had the chance anyway as things turned out. But I couldn't make him understand why I wouldn't say yes, and in the end I got annoyed and said something horrible to him. You know how you do – in the heat of the moment you say something you don't mean at all, and regret it straight away –?"

"Yes," Tamsin says, knowing all too well. "And you never saw him again to make it up?"

"Only for a few minutes. I went out to the airfield to wish him luck. We often did – WAAFs, groundcrew, whoever was off duty. But this time I was desperate to see him. There was usually a bit of hanging around before take-off. He came out from the plane in all his bulky flying gear. There wasn't time for a proper conversation. I just said, I'm sorry, and he said, It's all right, don't worry, and I'll see you tomorrow, and then he went. And that was the last time I ever saw him. I was on duty in flying control in the early hours of next morning and I watched the planes landing one by one and being marked off on the blackboard. There was a blank against his plane's code letter that would never be filled in. Missing. Him and the six others in the crew."

Tamsin pictures herself there, looking at the blank space. "Oh, Nan, how awful."

"Yes. And I can never forget that he went to his briefing straight from our argument. I've always wondered, suppose he was too upset or annoyed to listen properly? Supposing he missed some important detail? He was the navigator, you see . . . it was his responsibility to guide the pilot to the target and back. He was very good at it. But this time something went wrong."

"But people have rows all the time," Tamsin says, knowing that she would have felt exactly the same as Nan. "There could have been any number of reasons why his plane didn't come back."

Nan sighs. "I'll never know, will I?"

Tamsin thinks, this is one of the tragedies of war, this and thousands like it: not just the deaths but the unanswered questions, the unfinished conversations, the guilt that can never be forgotten; the maybes, the what-ifs, if only this or that hadn't happened.

Nan turns the page slowly and David's face is hidden.

"Charlie was wonderful to me," she says, "then, and always."

They have tea and Christmas cake and then Tamsin walks home slowly. She considers how many kinds of courage there are, physical and otherwise, and how deficient she is in all of them.

BOUQUET

On her return to E.T. Hall Tamsin finds Louise installed in Julia's old room. She has already imposed her own style on it by plastering the walls with posters and replacing the duvet cover with one of her own, in bold stripes.

"Come and celebrate my return from outer darkness," she invites Tamsin, and they indulge themselves on wine and shortbread which Louise has brought from home.

"This is a last fling, I want you to realise," Louise says with her mouth full. "It's definitely down to work for me. Starting first thing tomorrow. The finals are looming and I've hardly started on my dissertation yet. Actually it'll be a lot easier now that I've got a nice warm room to come back to. I used to hang about in the bar as an excuse not to go back to that freezing flat."

Tamsin is pleased to have her as a neighbour. Louise shuts herself firmly in her room for the first evening, but soon proves unable to resist distractions. On most nights, Tamsin, Louise, Josie and whoever else is around end up having coffee and chocolate biscuits, with which Louise is always supplied, and chatting till midnight. Louise's dissertation on Jacobean Tragedy crawls along, rarely advancing by more than one page per day.

"Whatever you do, don't get behind with your work," she warns Tamsin, who never does. "It makes it very difficult by the time you get to the third year." And she happily plugs in the kettle for another brew-up, her essay abandoned on the desk.

Tamsin resumes her swimming, goes to the film club with Tatsuya and joins a committee to organise a fund-raising concert for Rwanda. Every Sunday she and Louise go out walking, and Tamsin exchanges a few terse words with Jim if he's there. Quite frequently now he misses the Sunday walk to go rock-climbing in the Peak District with Dave or Glyn. Like Louise, he will be taking finals soon, although that doesn't seem to interfere with his outdoor activities. Louise, who is in the same group, says that he is even farther behind with his dissertation than she is.

Tamsin allows herself to feel superior; she can't imagine being so disorganised. She is working hard on her metals testing project, spending hours in the lab measuring tensile strength and ductility. Photographs taken under the scanning electron microscope reveal a fascinating new world in the fracture surfaces of metals. Tamsin gazes at the pictures in a far from scientific way, lost in contemplation. Wrought aluminium resembles meringue whipped into peaks; silicon carbide fibres are a forest of petrified stalks; titanium is an aerial view of mountain summits and ridges, Helvellyns and Striding Edges... Less fancifully, she turns her mind to a more methodical analysis of fracture behaviour. *Commercially pure titanium: cup and cone fracture is typical of a ductile metal*, she writes.

The fund-raising gig for Rwanda is on the top floor of the Union building. Tamsin has been deputed to serve behind the bar, on the basis of being quick at mental arithmetic rather than through any previous barmaiding experience. Harry has organised the band, a local rock group called Nightrider, who have agreed to do the gig in return for free drinks and a plug on local radio. Their amplifiers are turned up so high that Tamsin feels she is being crushed behind a solid wall of sound, every sane thought driven out of her head; occasionally the mesmeric thumping is varied with a high-pitched metallic whine that sets her teeth on edge. The room is in darkness, with strobe lighting, so that the forms of dancers flicker like shapes cut out of paper. She resigns herself to temporary brain-damage: stand back and think of Rwanda. People lurch eerily towards the bar table and open their mouths soundlessly, like goldfish, and she tries to guess what they want. Any complicated request, like "Can you change a twenty-pound note?" or "What kind of lager have you got?" means taking part in an elaborate strobe-lit dumb-show, a performance art in its own right.

After the first hour or so she decides that her head is going to explode if she doesn't get out of here for five minutes. She is attempting to convey to Daniel, her partner at the bar, that she is going outside for a breath of silence, when someone lurches up looking like Frankenstein's monster, with eye-sockets and cheekbones carved into deep shadow. Tamsin stares, and recognises Whistler.

He bellows something at her. Automatically she reaches for a beer-bottle and opener, but Whistler shakes his head and gesticulates, and she understands that he is asking her to dance. She doesn't like dancing, not to this sort of stuff, but she does like Whistler, so she mimes "Back in a minute" to Daniel and joins the gyrating mass of flung arms and whirling bodies. She never quite knows what to do with herself, but it's hardly going to matter greatly with such limited visibility, so she jigs about a bit and laughs at Whistler, whose loose jerking movements make him look like a stringed puppet. Soon he puts a hand on her shoulder and shouts into her ear. She can make out just one word: "erroneous". Or perhaps it was "acrimonious" or even "Polonius"; she shakes her head to show that she has no idea what he's on about, and Whistler takes her hand and pulls her towards the door. Gratefully she follows him out to the landing and they lean on the railing at the top of the stairs. From here, the music is only a heavy bass thump which makes the whole building vibrate.

Tamsin's ears begin to recover slightly. "I wouldn't have thought this was your sort of occasion," she shouts at Whistler. The words float from somewhere deep inside her skull and echo in the stairwell.

"It isn't," Whistler shouts back. "Thought I'd better support the good cause. But I'm leaving now that I've paid for my ticket and had a token dance."

"What were you trying to say in there?"

"Not the ideal conditions for trying to raise a delicate matter, I admit."

Following him through a mixture of lip-reading and ear-straining, Tamsin shouts, "Would it be a good idea to move farther away?"

"Highly advisable, I think."

They retreat downstairs and sit side by side on the bottom step where they can hear each other, and Tamsin asks, "What delicate matter?"

"You may think this is a cheek," Whistler says, "but I can't help wishing that you and Jim could overlook your difference of opinion. I speak as a mere onlooker, but it seems a pity that one argument should end a relationship that seemed so satisfactory to both parties."

Tamsin opens her mouth to reply, but Whistler says, "You may well say it's none of my business. You're quite right, but I do hate to see the lad moping about. A simple, amiable soul is our Jim in many ways, but he does take things to heart. And I do have a vested interest in his mental well-being. I'm fed up with tripping over his feet and his essay notes while he stares at the same page day after day."

"I don't see what it's got to do with me," Tamsin says stiffly. "He's been stuck on his dissertation ever since I've known him."

"I know you feel badly about what happened on Striding Edge," Whistler says, "but it was entirely Jim's fault, not yours. He knows it was, and that's why he feels so bad about it. He should have known what conditions would be like in that sort of weather and he should have given you a clearer idea of what to expect. Exposed places like that can be scary, especially if you're new to it."

"It'd always be scary for me, never mind the weather," Tamsin says. "Jim should have realised I'm a pathetic coward, is what you mean. I'm terrified of heights."

Whistler shrugs. "Does that matter? We all have our weaknesses. Fiona goes into hysterics if there's a spider in the bath. Why don't I go rock-climbing with Jim and Dave? Because I'd be scared out of my socks, that's why. A little danger can be exciting but too much danger is dangerous. The art is in knowing where to draw the line."

"Well, anyway," Tamsin says doubtfully, "I suppose Jim can speak for himself?"

"I wish he would."

She considers this. Whistler means well but he's probably got it wrong; after all, Jim has shown no sign of further interest since she rebuffed him so successfully. Whistler doesn't know quite how vile she was.

"Where is he?" she asks. "He didn't come with you?"

"No. I left him in glum and solitary contemplation of *The Playboy of the Western World*." Whistler looks at his watch. "I must go and find Fiona. See you on the walk tomorrow?"

He goes out into the darkness. Tamsin sits on the stairs for a few moments longer, not sure what Whistler is suggesting: was he hinting that she should go round and see Jim now? But she couldn't, even if she wanted to: there is Daniel on his own at the bar, and everything to clear up after the concert. And, quite apart from that, she has failed once and doesn't want to risk failing again.

The following day's outing is a coach trip to the Hope Valley. Getting ready, Tamsin is surprised to find Louise up early, filling her flask in the kitchen.

"You're coming? I thought you were going to spend the day deep in revenge tragedy."

"Mustn't overdo it," Louise says airily, screwing up her Thermos lid. "Fresh air and exercise will be a lot more inspiring than staring at a blank sheet of paper. But I'm making you personally responsible for supervising five hours of solid work every evening, starting tomorrow."

"I'm beginning to think," Tamsin says, "that it would be far less trouble if I wrote the damned thing for you."

They go down to the coach. After Whistler's match-making attempt, Tamsin is half-relieved to find that Jim isn't coming today: either rock-climbing or the dissertation must have claimed his attention.

"Seen this?" Louise passes her a printed leaflet. "I picked it up ages ago when we were at Edale. It's only three weeks away but they've still got places."

Tamsin reads: *Walking for Women, a weekend in the Lake District, based at Patterdale Youth Hostel.*

"If I aim to finish my dissertation by then, I could give myself the weekend as a reward," Louise explains. "Would you fancy coming? You said you wanted to go back to the Lake District."

"Yes, I do. Who else is going?"

"No one yet. I thought a weekend with only women might be rather nice without blokes talking about Hard Severes and making it macho and tough. I could ask Candida," Louise says, "but somehow I don't think she'd fancy a whole weekend without male interest."

Tamsin looks at the leaflet again and decides. "Oh yes, let's go. It'll be fun."

Louise works solidly, and on Saturday morning instructs Tamsin not to let her out of her room until she's finished. The day is wet, dull and gloomy; Josie is out on a theatre visit, Liz is away for the weekend, and the corridor is quiet. Tamsin decides to spend the morning catching up on washing and letters. She sits on her bed biting the end of her pen and watching rain wash diagonally over the window-pane. There isn't much temptation to go out, but she will probably go over to see Rikayah later and suggest a game of badminton. Louise can't seriously expect her to act as jailer for the entire day.

She hears the tread of footsteps in the corridor and then the rap of knuckles on someone's door farther along. Someone answers and then Tamsin hears a conversation between Louise and a male voice. Louise isn't going to be allowed to work undisturbed after all.

But Louise is evidently firmer than Tamsin expected, because a few moments later the door closes again and the footsteps come to her end of the corridor. There is a pause and then a brisk knocking on her door.

"Come in," she answers.

In the doorway, very wet, dressed as usual in

his green waterproof and with hair plastered to his forehead, stands Jim.

"Hello," he says cheerfully. "I came over to borrow Louise's *Dictionary of Literary Terms*" – he holds up the book as evidence – "but she's busy working and sent me away. She said you were in so I've come to say hello."

"Hello." Tamsin is pleased that her voice doesn't come out as a ridiculous squeak. They look at each other guardedly. Jim shouldn't *do* this, Tamsin thinks; bursting in without warning just isn't *fair*. "Would you like some coffee?" she asks, for something to say while her stomach returns to its proper place. "I wonder if Louise –"

"Yes, please. But I don't think Louise wants to be interrupted. She was beavering away like a maniac."

"Are you going to take your coat off? You're dripping on the rug."

Jim showers her with water as he takes off his coat and hangs it behind the door, and then sits down on the bed. She takes mugs and a jar of Nescafé out of the cupboard and goes along the corridor, past Louise's firmly shut door, to the kitchen, remembering that Jim likes his coffee black with sugar. She wonders whether Whistler and Louise have been conspiring.

"Are you sure this isn't an excuse not to work on your dissertation?" she says lightly when she comes back.

Jim looks hurt. "I've nearly finished it. It's

taken me ages but I've only got the bibliography and footnotes to do."

"Oh, Whistler said – Whistler said you were stuck." She sits down at her desk, turning the chair to face him.

"Well, I have been. But I'm not stuck now. I've worked on it like fury for the last month. The trouble with Whistler," he says self-righteously, "is that he can't tell the difference between vacancy and deep contemplation."

"So now it's just the finals," Tamsin says. It is only a matter of weeks before Jim takes his exams and leaves.

He grins. "Not much of a *just* about it."

"No. Sorry."

"I'm sorry too."

Tamsin looks at him, not sure what he means. He puts his mug on the floor and reaches for her hand, holding it in both of his.

"About that stupid row," he says. "It was all my fault."

"No, it wasn't. It was mine. I was horrible."

"I don't blame you. You *were* horrible, but you were quite right." Jim pauses, and then adds tentatively, "Could you –" at the same moment as Tamsin says, "Yes, but I –"

"Go on," Jim says.

"No, you."

"I was going to say," Jim says, "could you possibly come and sit here, next to me? I feel as if I'm being interviewed."

Tamsin tries to remember that she isn't sure whether she wants to get involved again, but all the same she moves over and arranges herself carefully, though not too close. Jim shuffles nearer and puts both arms round her. His grey sweater is rough and slightly scratchy, and smells familiar. "Tamsin!" he says softly. "I've missed you so much. Couldn't we –"

At that point there is a loud rapping on the door. Jim grimaces, and Tamsin moves a little apart and says, "That'll be Louise. Come in," she calls reluctantly.

The door opens to admit a huge sheaf of flowers: lilies, tulips, irises, wrapped in rain-spattered cellophane and tied with a flourish of pink ribbon. Tamsin and Jim stare in astonishment, and then a smiling face follows the bouquet into the room. Tamsin's father.

He hands the flowers to Tamsin, who is too amazed to take them, so he lays them on the desk. "I had quite a job to find where you are," he remarks, as if Tamsin had asked him to come. "A fair old maze, this place. Nice room you've got here." He looks at Jim. "Oh, is this the boyfriend? Pleased to meet you."

"Jim," Tamsin says. "Jim, this is Paul Strivener."

She deliberately does not say *my father*; Jim will know who he is. They both stare at Paul. He looks different today, out of his business suit. He is wearing smart casual clothes: a waxed coat, cords and a petrol-blue sweatshirt. His well-heeled presence has invaded Tamsin's room; him and his flowers. Tamsin scrambles to her feet, and Jim stands too. Paul raises his eyebrows, looks Jim up and down and says roguishly to Tamsin, "Sorry, have I interrupted something?"

"Yes, you have. What do you want?" Tamsin says. She hopes Paul can't see that she is trembling. Jim gazes at her in surprise and she realises that until now he must have thought she had been expecting her father to turn up.

"Just popped up to see you, like I said I would," Paul says. "It's not far up the motorway. Thought I'd take you out for lunch. Do you know anywhere?"

"No, thanks," Tamsin says. "I'm going out with Jim."

Paul spreads out both hands in a no-problem gesture. "You're welcome to come along too, Jim."

"Thank you," Jim says coldly, "but I think Tamsin's saying no."

Paul looks from Jim to Tamsin, his face expressing annoyance. He seems different today, brash, confident, more like the glimpse Tamsin had of him in the showroom, and she feels far less sympathetic towards this version than to the downcast, penitent one. He wants to play the affluent father, providing lunch and flowers, accommodating hangers-on.

"Come on now, Tam, be reasonable," he says. "I've come a long way specially to see you."

"It's taken you eighteen years," she retorts. "I told you, I don't want to see you again. And neither does Mum. How could you phone her like that as if nothing had happened? Did you really think she'd greet you with open arms? Don't you realise how it upset her?"

Paul takes a step back, looking offended. "I meant well. Naturally it was a bit of a shock for Abby. How was I to know you'd kept our meeting a secret from her?"

"Don't try to make it my fault! Anyway, it must be clear by now that Mum doesn't want anything to do with you, and I don't want you coming here. Leave us alone, both of us."

"Don't be silly, Tam. There's no need to fly off the handle." Paul sits down at Tamsin's desk and gives Jim a man-to-man look which means *Aren't women awkward*. "Would you mind, Jim, if I had a chat with Tamsin in private? This is all a bit difficult. I've come a long way and we haven't seen much of each other . . ."

"I'm not going unless Tamsin asks me to," Jim says.

Tamsin glances at him and tells Paul, "Anything you want to say to me, Jim can hear. But I don't think there's much point. I'd prefer it if you left."

Paul tries one of his charming smiles. "Now come on, Tamsin, you can't really mean that!

Let's have a chat over lunch. I know how you must feel –"

"No," Tamsin says. "You don't. And you obviously don't understand how my mother feels, either."

Paul's smile wavers and fades. "I thought you might be a bit more reasonable. After all, you did make the first move. I don't think you're being fair. Not fair at all."

"*Oh* – how can you talk about being fair? After you –" The words stick in Tamsin's throat, threatening to choke her. Jim moves a little closer to Paul, ominously, like a bouncer. Paul gets slowly to his feet and gives Tamsin a reproachful look as he moves towards the door.

"Strikes me it'd be a good idea for all concerned if you knew what you wanted," he offers as a parting shot. "I thought maybe you had more sense than your mother. But I was wrong."

"Don't forget these." Tamsin grabs the bouquet of flowers and shoves them at him. "They must be for your wife."

He turns abruptly and goes out, shutting the door firmly behind him. Tamsin daren't look at Jim. She leans against the door and listens until her father's footsteps retreat along the corridor and the fire door slams shut. Her adrenalin rush has subsided and she feels shaky, as if her legs might give way. No longer angry, she feels only doubt: *was* she unreasonable and unfair? Did she really mean to reject her father so forcefully? And what must Jim think of her, now that she has shown herself at her nastiest again?

"I'm sorry about that," she says. She fears bursting into tears if she says any more.

Jim hesitates and then takes her coat and his from the peg. "Come on! We're going out."

"What do you mean? Where?" She submits to being helped on with her coat. "What if he comes back? I feel as if my room's polluted . . ."

"I don't think he will, and in any case he won't find us if we're not here. You said we were going out to lunch, and we are – if you meant it?"

"Yes?"

Jim picks up her room keys from the desk. "I can't offer the degree of opulence he probably had in mind, but what would you say to a sandwich from Marks and Spencer's and feeding the ducks in the park?"

She closes her eyes. "Sounds great."

It is wet and cold, hardly the day for sauntering in the park, but they find a shelter close to the deserted lake. A few ducks paddle over hopefully.

"If I'd had any idea what I was stirring up when I went to look for him," Tamsin says, "I wouldn't have done it."

"Yes, you would," Jim says. "You needed to know. I know you don't like all you've found out, but now you can – well, not exactly forget about him, but accept it. He's him and you're you. You might have his genes, but that doesn't make you the same sort of person."

"Accept that my father's a –" She hesitates, not at all sure how to describe him. "Well, not quite as much of a monster as I expected, I suppose. But he's *weak*. That's what surprises me. I always thought of him as the dominant one, making the decisions, stringing my mother along, but the point is that *she's* the stronger one. All he did was run away when things got difficult."

Like I do, she thinks. My father's not like Jim. He's like me.

"Do you think I've seen the last of him?" she asks.

There is a pause while Jim throws bits of crust to the mallards, and then he says, "Well, perhaps not. You might feel a bit differently about it when it's sunk in. You might even want to keep in touch. Because – well, he is your father, and you can't just forget about that, now that you know. And he's a bit pathetic, isn't he, from what you say? He's messed up his own life even more than your mother's."

"I suppose so." Tamsin can't help thinking that she's the pathetic one.

"But it must be on your own terms, not his," Jim says. "He hasn't got any rights over you."

"No. I think that's what frightens Mum so much – she's always thought he'll try to get me away from her. But of course he couldn't, not now." Tamsin watches the scrabbling ducks. She reflects that she knows very little about Jim's parents; he rarely mentions his family, though she knows he has an older brother. "What's your father like?"

Jim makes a wry face. "I don't get on with him an awful lot better than you do with yours. I'm a big disappointment to him."

"Why?"

"Because he thinks I'm wasting my time doing an English degree. Literature is for poofters, that's his attitude. He's a builder, got his own business, and he wanted me to go in with him at sixteen. That's what Sean did, my brother. We had a big argument when I wanted to stay on for A-levels, let alone a degree. When I go home, it's always *When are you going to stop scrounging and get yourself a proper job*? As for financial support, he made it clear from the start that I wasn't going to get a single penny from him. He'd see me give up first. That's why I took a year out before I started, to save as much as I could."

Tamsin stares at the ruffled surface of the lake. She can't imagine it, always having had full support from her family. "What did you do?"

"Bricklaying. With one of his rivals." Jim smiles. "One of the advantages of coming from a line of Irish navvies. I sometimes do it as a holiday job as well."

"What about your mother? What does she think?"

"She just wants to keep the peace, but she'd never dare go against the old man."

Tamsin looks at him with new respect. "And you told me you were aimless – you drifted into it. That doesn't sound much like drifting."

"Oh, well . . The ironic thing is, Dad would be quite happy if I'd done Engineering, like you. He'd see some point in that."

Much later, they walk back to campus in the gloom of a wet Saturday evening.

"One thing that puzzles me," Tamsin remarks, "is why it nearly always rains when I'm with you. I've come to expect it. Any friend of yours needs good waterproofs."

Jim twirls round a lamp-post and links his arm through hers. "It's the pathetic fallacy in reverse. We're happy, so it's raining."

It has been the strangest day Tamsin can re-member. She feels out of touch with reality; time hardly matters, she and Jim have wandered from place to place, talking, talking, getting wet and not minding. In spite of the traumas and surprises of the day she does feel happy, in an uncertain, tremulous mood that feels a bit like being drunk, as if when she is sober everything will seem dull and ordinary again. For all her intention of not getting romantically involved again, she feels so grateful to Jim for his support today – for being *there* – that it's hard to think about him with the planned degree of detachment. Outside the hall of residence he stops by the dripping laurel bushes and kisses her, his face wet and cold against hers.

"I missed you, too," she murmurs, picking up their interrupted conversation from hours ago.

"Good. I don't see why I should suffer on my own," Jim says, and then, more seriously, "This isn't just for today, is it? I mean, we're going to carry on seeing each other?"

"That seems a good idea to me . . . don't you think?"

"When, though? I won't be around tomorrow – I've arranged to go climbing with Dave, and I can't let him down at short notice."

"Even if the weather's like this?"

"All the more fun," Jim says. "You know Dave. It would take gale force twelve and an earthquake, both at once, to make him even think about putting it off."

"Oh, I know. He has to twist your arm to get you to go at all," Tamsin teases.

"Shall I come and see you when I get back?" Jim suggests.

Tamsin doesn't think she can wait that long. She has an inspiration. "What about seven in the morning at the swimming pool?"

"Er, no. I don't think that's a very good idea."

"Oh, go on! Just because it's Sunday doesn't mean you can't get up for seven."

"No, that's not the problem," Jim says. "It's just that I can't swim."

TESTS

On Thursday evening, when someone comes up to her room to call her to the ground floor telephone, Tamsin's first thought is that it must be Paul again.

"Was it a male voice?" she asks.

"No, a woman."

Mum, then, but they usually speak to each other at the weekend. Tamsin runs down the two flights of stairs and arrives breathless.

"I thought I'd better let you know," Abigail's voice says, "that Mum's gone into hospital today for more tests."

"Oh no!" Tamsin's voice comes out tight and flat. "What sort of tests?"

"Routine tests, they're calling them. She's been having a lot of stomach pains lately and hasn't got much appetite. They've taken her in now to see if she needs an operation."

"I'll come home for the weekend," Tamsin says. "Tomorrow night."

"Oh, I don't think there's any need to panic. I'd let you know if there was any urgent reason to come home."

But it *must* be urgent, Tamsin thinks. People wait weeks, months, for hospital tests and operations on the National Health. If Nan has been taken in so suddenly it must be because of serious concern. She insists, and eventually Abigail gives way.

"All right, then. Phone when you get to the station and I'll pick you up. Don't walk home on your own at that time of night."

Back in her room, Tamsin looks up train times and throws a few things into her rucksack. She plans to leave straight after tomorrow's lab session; there's a train that will get her home by about ten. Her weekend plans will have to be shelved – she was going leafleting with the Animal Rights group on Saturday afternoon and to the cinema with Jim in the evening. Sorting coins, she goes down to the phone again and rings the flat. To her relief it is Jim who answers.

"I'll come with you if you like," he offers.

Tamsin thinks about it. It would be nice to have his company, but on the other hand this is a family crisis – albeit a minor one, according to Mum.

"Thanks," she says. "I appreciate it, but I think I ought to go on my own. Anyway, you can't let Dave down for climbing on Sunday. I'll come and see you when I get back, shall I?"

To get home she has to catch an Inter-City train into London and a local one out to Hertfordshire. Arriving at the station, she telephones home and then watches out for Abigail's red Golf, but is surprised to see her mother waving from the passenger seat of a strange car. Abigail gets out, kisses Tamsin and opens the back door for her, and says, "This is Roger."

The driver turns round and says, "Hi, Tamsin," but it is too dark to make out more than the shape of his head. Roger? Tamsin can't remember hearing about a Roger. Presumably he has replaced Henry as the latest Lonely Heart.

"We've been to the hospital this evening," Abigail explains. "Mum was fine, looking forward to seeing you tomorrow."

We've been to the hospital? What exactly is going on here?

Instead of going straight home, Roger drives into town and stops outside the Chinese takeaway. "There wasn't time to cook," Abigail says. "And you must be starving. Come in and help me choose."

"Who's this Roger then?" Tamsin asks while they wait at the counter for their order. "I haven't heard of him before, have I?"

"Yes, you have. He's the one writing the book, you know, the one about the RAF and the war, that Nan's been helping him with. We told you about it at Christmas."

"Oh yes. The freelance journalist," Tamsin

says. "For a minute I thought he was one of your Lonely Hearts."

"Well, yes, in a way he . . ."

Tamsin looks at her mother sharply. Her hair has swung forward over her cheek as she leans on the counter, but underneath she is definitely blushing.

"Mum!"

"I haven't known him all that long," Abigail says, "only since you went back after Christmas. He seemed to get on very well with Mum. I met him a couple of times when he was round there, and one night he took both of us out for a meal."

"And?"

"And, he phoned me a couple of days later and . . . well, we've been seeing each other since then. He's very nice, you'll see."

Tamsin can't help laughing, and Abigail frowns. "I don't know what's so funny about it," she says sternly. "Teenagers don't have all the fun. I'm not completely over the hill, you know."

"No, I know! It struck me as funny that after all that advertising and box-number business and being interviewed by no-hopers, you end up meeting someone through your own mother. You are a dark horse, not telling me! What happened to Henry, anyway?"

"Oh, Henry," Abigail says as if she can hardly remember who he is. "Far too charming for his own good. He had a shortlist of about fifteen women and he was working his way through them. When he's done that he'll probably start all over again."

"So you've finished with the Lonely Hearts?"

"It's far too early to say," Abigail says primly.

Over the meal, Tamsin studies Roger discreetly. She is relieved to see that he is not in the least like Paul, having been half-afraid that her mother's tastes might subconsciously run in that direction. He is older than Abigail, Tamsin guesses in his early forties; slim, greying a little, with an intelligent, humorous face and a ready smile. He seems quite at home in the house, she notices; he and Abigail have an affectionate teasing manner with each other.

"How are you getting on with the book?" Tamsin asks him, and he pulls a face.

"I've had all the fun," he says, "going round meeting people, visiting wartime airfields, even getting inside a Lancaster bomber on one occasion. Now it's time for the solid graft. Writing is such bloody awful hard *work*. There's no end to the distractions you can find rather than face a blank word processor screen."

"Clearing out his sock drawer," Abigail mocks; "playing with the cat, sorting all his ancient LPs into alphabetical order . . ."

"Abigail's good for me," Roger says. "She makes me get down to regular work, gives me a proper sense of discipline."

Regular work, discipline? *Mum?* Can we be talking about the same person, Tamsin wonders.

She is sure they are holding hands under the table. She smiles and eats her sweet and sour vegetables, feeling like an indulgent parent.

Abigail and Tamsin visit Nan on Saturday afternoon. The ward is a smaller one than last time, smelling of daffodils and talcum powder. When they arrive Nan is sitting on a chair beside her bed, fully dressed and reading the book Tamsin gave her for Christmas. She is determinedly cheerful, as if embarrassed at finding herself the centre of so much attention.

"You shouldn't have come all this way home in the middle of term," she scolds Tamsin. "I hope it wasn't for my benefit?"

She looks very small beside the high hospital bed, washed out by the surrounding whiteness; her hazel eyes are the only spots of colour in her face. Sometimes it seems to Tamsin that Nan is getting younger as well as older. Her expression is sweet, girlish, bringing to mind the face above the Greek costume in *A Midsummer Night's Dream*. Nan has always looked delicate.

"So you've met Roger? A nice young man, isn't he?"

They chat about Roger, the book, Tamsin's course, Aunt Rachel's forthcoming holiday in France: everything, it seems, but the one reason they are all here, Nan's illness. It is a taboo subject. Everyone knows it's there, lurking among them like an unwelcome visitor, but they are all ignoring it in the hope that it will give up and creep away by itself. All Nan says is, "I expect they'll send me home on Monday. Don't you worry, Tamsin love."

"I'll be home again for Easter in a couple of weeks," Tamsin says.

A tea-trolley clatters along the ward and a pretty young nurse brings Nan her cup. "Milk and no sugar, Mrs Fox, just the way you like it. I'll pop it up here on your cabinet, where you can reach it, shall I?"

Tamsin wants to shout out: *This is my grandmother, she's not an imbecile! You don't have to talk to her as if she's senile, slow-witted!* She doesn't want to leave Nan here alone. Without her family for support she will be rendered anonymous, an item to be processed and sent home. Or not sent home.

Driving home with her mother, Tamsin learns that there is a possibility of exploratory surgery.

"Of course it might be something straightforward," Abigail says brightly.

Or it might not.

"Don't start imagining the worst." Abigail gives her a sidelong look. "I know what a worrier you are. Perhaps I shouldn't have rung you, but you did make me promise."

Tamsin does not dare to use the word hanging in the air between them. Cancer. The big C. It might turn out to be cancer. Her mind races uncontrollably. If it – the worst, which no one actually names – happens, Mum will have Roger around to support her; and then she is frightened for allowing herself to think in such terms.

Her first experience of death was when William, Nan and Grandad's black-and-white cat, had to be put to sleep. For as long as Tamsin could remember, William had been around: a big fat cat, patrolling the garden, sleeping in his favourite sunny places, turning up without fail at mealtimes and eating hugely. He was scrupulous about washing and kept the white parts of his fur snowy clean. Tamsin always knew William's age because it was the same as her own. Now, at eleven, William quite suddenly became old and ill. His food was barely touched, his coat looked coarse and he dribbled milk down his front. He would sit in one place all day, hardly venturing outside the back door. He looked thinner every time Tamsin saw him. She hated to see him like that. Surely the fat sleek version of William must still be around somewhere?

"As long as he's getting some enjoyment out of life," Nan would say; but soon it became apparent that William wasn't. His back legs wobbled when he got out of his basket and his miaow became a pitiful wail.

It was Nan who took William to the vet, because Grandad Charlie couldn't face it. Tamsin and her mother were there when Nan came back sniffing and red-eyed with the empty cat-basket.

"What did they do to him?" Tamsin asked, morbidly curious.

"It was very peaceful, love," Nan said. "William wouldn't have known anything about it. The vet clipped a bit of fur from his front leg and gave him the injection to put him to sleep. William was purring, then he slowly went limp. By the time the needle came out of his leg, he was dead. Dear old William," she said sadly. "He was a lovely cat. We'll miss him."

They all looked at the place in front of the fire where William liked to sit. Tamsin thought of William's big green eyes glazing over.

"Cats are lucky," Nan said. "I'd like to go as peacefully as that when my turn comes."

"Oh, *Mum*," Tamsin's mum said. She couldn't bear anyone talking about illness or death. "Don't say things like that."

On Saturday evening, when Abigail, Roger and Tamsin are playing Trivial Pursuit, the phone rings in Abigail's bedroom. She goes to answer it and then pokes her head round the door.

"It's for you," she tells Tamsin. "Someone called Jim."

Tamsin and Jim have such a long conversation that the Trivial Pursuit is abandoned when she comes back, and Abigail and Roger are in the kitchen washing up.

"Now who's the dark horse?" Abigail teases. "Is this the one you were keen on before?"

"Yes," Tamsin admits.

"So it's all on again then?" Abigail prompts.

"Yes, I suppose it is, really."

"He's got a nice voice."

"Yes."

Abigail gives up, and looks appealingly at Roger. "Forthcoming, isn't she, my daughter? Isn't it an enormous privilege to be kept so fully informed? I thought communication skills were part of your course," she says to Tamsin.

"You can talk," Tamsin jokes back, "considering that at my age you'd left home without so much as a –" She catches her breath in confusion, flushing hotly as she realises what a clomping great foot she has just put in it.

"It's all right!" Abigail rushes over and gives her a hug. "Roger knows all about it."

Later, in bed, Tamsin thinks about this and finds it enormously reassuring. Mum wouldn't have told Roger about her past if she didn't feel she could trust him, and Tamsin feels instinctively that the relationship will work out. She hears Roger leaving, very late, and suspects that he would normally stay the night. She is surprised to find that she doesn't mind at all.

By mid-afternoon on Sunday Tamsin is on the train heading north. She has brought a book to read, but can't concentrate. It has been a mixed sort of weekend, anxiety about Nan alternating with pleasure at seeing her mother so happy with

Roger. Now she is looking forward to seeing Jim; she hopes he will be back from climbing early. She wants him so badly that the hours of the journey stretch out interminably.

She walks from the station, deciding to go up to her room first to dump her bag and have a quick wash before going round to the flat. The wind is cold tonight, from the north, finding the gaps in her clothing and making her ears ache. Inside the hall of residence she runs upstairs two at a time. Her corridor is in darkness, no lights showing under any of the doors. At her own door, a folded slip of paper has been tucked into the name-plate.

Phone message from Dave, it says in handwriting she doesn't recognise. *Jim's had an accident, St Luke's Casualty department.*

Tamsin is down the stairs and hurrying back to the city centre before she has thought clearly about what she is doing. Her imagination supplies pictures of countless different climbing accidents: a slip, a rockfall, a failed belay, a mistake when scrambling unroped, a handhold giving way . . . She sees Jim falling into space, pitching down a sheer drop, other climbers staring appalled at the broken body . . . She feels sick, shaken, as if she is the one who's fallen. If only Dave had left a clearer message so that she knew just how bad it was . . . She has *known* this will happen, *expected* it; it has to happen if she allows herself to love Jim. It is fated, part of the pattern. If it hadn't happened now it would be in the Alps, the Cairngorms, the Pyrenees, the Cuillins . . .

Only when she is on the bus to St Luke's does it occur to her that it would have been a good idea to phone the flat first; Scott or Whistler must know what's happened by now. She has no clear idea where St Luke's is, but the bus carries her through darkness to the outer edge of the city, by the ring road, and deposits her in front of a modern complex of buildings intersected by floodlit concrete paths and covered walkways. There is a signpost board at the entrance with arrows pointing in all directions. Tamsin's eyes dart to the word *Casualty* and she enters a hospital for the second time that day.

She dashes along polished corridors, her footsteps echoing. In a minute she will be there and she will know. She doesn't want to know. She wants to hang on to these last few moments of ignorance and hope . . . Swing doors close behind her as she enters the Casualty department and looks wildly around at the reception area. There is no Jim, no Dave, no prone forms on stretchers, only a woman with a child mournfully cradling a cut hand.

A nurse comes out of a door behind the desk and smiles at Tamsin pleasantly. "Yes?"

"I'm looking for Jim McGrath – James," Tamsin gasps. "He was brought in earlier. A rock-climbing accident."

"McGrath . . . McGrath . . ." The nurse's fore-finger moves down a list, maddeningly slow. "Yes. Here we are. A broken arm and concussion. He's being kept in overnight."

Tamsin's head swims with relief as she registers that it isn't a fatal or even a very serious injury. "Where is he? Can I see him?"

The nurse looks at her list again and then at the clock above the desk. "Beech Ward. But I don't suppose you'll be allowed in, not tonight. Visiting's over for today."

Tamsin runs off again into the maze of identical corridors and walkways, climbing two flights of stairs and arriving at Beech Ward just as the last visitors are leaving. Seeing that a nurse is waiting to close the door behind them, Tamsin rushes up and inserts herself into the gap.

"Please let me come in!"

"Sorry," the nurse says firmly. "Visiting finished at half-past seven."

"Oh, please! Just for five minutes!" Tamsin is desperate. She *must* see Jim; she can't go back until she does. If she doesn't see him for herself she won't be able to believe that he isn't dead, or horribly injured; the Casualty nurse could have made a mistake.

"Who have you come to see?"

"James McGrath. He's been brought in today with a broken arm and concussion."

The nurse nods. "I know who you mean. Are you his girlfriend?"

Tamsin nods, and the nurse's expression softens. "All right, then, but it really will have to be five minutes or you'll get me into trouble. Second bed from the end, on the left."

"Oh, thank you!"

Tamsin scuttles in before the nurse can change her mind. Male faces look at her curiously as she walks past the rows of beds. She can't imagine Jim in a place like this, all neat and orderly; but there he is, sitting up in bed, staring into space and looking extremely fed up. He is wearing a blue pyjama jacket with one sleeve hanging empty, his right arm plastered and in a sling.

"Jim –!"

He looks round, and his eyes swim into focus on her face. "Oh, how did you –?" He reaches out his left arm to hug her as best he can and she bends down to kiss him, avoiding the sling.

"What *happened*?" She is dizzy with gratitude that he is here, warm and alive and still recognisably Jim.

"Sit round the other side," he says, moving his legs aside so that she can sit down on the bed, "and then you needn't worry about this useless appendage. Oh, come here . . ."

After a few moments Tamsin disentangles herself, realising that patients in the neighbouring beds are watching with interest. "Careful! I'm sure this sort of thing isn't allowed. Especially out of visiting hours. Oh, Jim, what happened?" she asks again. "Was it a bad fall?"

Jim looks at her warily. "Dave didn't tell you?"

"No, I haven't spoken to Dave. Someone left a message saying you'd had an accident – it didn't say how bad – I thought –"

"Oh, God," Jim says, understanding. "I'm sorry. You've had a rough weekend, one way and another. I told him to tell you not to worry. They're only keeping me in because of mild concussion."

"It doesn't matter, now that I'm here – but tell me what *happened*!" She can't understand Jim's reticence. He looks definitely sheepish.

"Well," he says. "For a start, it wasn't a climbing accident at all."

"But what –"

"The climbing was fine," Jim says. "Haven't I always told you we don't take unnecessary risks? We finished early and left Matlock at about two, because I wanted to be back before you. Then we stopped at a service station for petrol and some drinks, and I didn't notice the floor was wet and I went flying. And crashed my head against a display stand for good measure."

"Oh, *Jim*!" Tamsin collapses against him, laughing, even though she knows a broken arm isn't at all funny whether you do it falling off a precipice or falling over your own feet. "You *idiot*!"

Jim's face spreads slowly into a rueful grin. "Oddly enough, I thought you might say that.

That's why I made the most of the sympathy while it lasted. I'm going to feel a right prat, aren't I, walking about with this sling and having to explain to everyone how I did it . . ."

"Does it hurt awfully?"

"It hurt like hell until Dave got me here, but now I'm drugged up to the eyeballs. Can you tell?"

"You do look a bit bleary. At least it's your right arm," she says, Jim being left-handed. "You'll still be able to do your finals."

"Well, I'll look forward to that," Jim says drily. "But first I've got to think of something to tell Scott and Whistler and Glyn. Do you think you could drop hints about me falling down a crevasse in the Peruvian Andes and struggling single-handed back to base camp . . . ?"

"I'll start spreading it about right away."

"And how was your Nan?"

Tamsin tells him, until she notices the nurse signalling to her and pointing at the clock. "My time's up. I'll have to go now. How are you getting back tomorrow?"

"Dave's coming for me in the van."

"I'll see you tomorrow evening, then?" She kisses him and stands up reluctantly. "And do be careful not to trip over anything in the meantime. Stairs can be very tricky."

HEIGHTS

"*A*n A! How do you do it?"

Rikayah stares at the grade written at the end of Tamsin's fracture surface assignment. Tamsin gazes at it too, thinking there must have been some mistake; but no, there isn't even a minus sign after it to diminish the glory. Her hard work has paid off. ("I suppose you'd have liked to stick my poor shattered bones under the microscope," Jim said, provoking the response, "Of course. Why do you think I came rushing over to the hospital?")

Her first A. She is beginning to realise that it isn't going to be a question of struggling through the summer exams in order to make it to the second year; more a question of aiming for the top. The only other student to get an A for the project is Tatsuya, but she has always known that Tatsuya is brilliant. She is well aware that it's all down to hard grind in her case.

They start on water engineering that week,

which is where Tamsin thinks her main interest will lie when it comes to specialising later. There will be her summer work in industry, then, at the end of the course, a job overseas . . . She finds herself wondering, What about Jim? Is he going to be in the picture? What will happen after he leaves in June? She remembers how she used to rail at Becky: *You're far too young to tie yourself down to one person; you're going to have all sorts of opportunities; surely you don't want to limit your chances just because you won't leave Greg?*

It's not like that with Jim and me, she tells herself. There is no suggestion of tying themselves down; neither of them has so much as mentioned what will happen after Jim's finals. But June is not far off, a matter of weeks; she is alarmed to realise what a big gap there will be in her life when Jim leaves.

On Thursday evening Josie asks her to make up a four for badminton with Rikayah and Griselda.

"Sorry, I can't," Tamsin says. "I'm going with Jim to get the shopping for the flat. He can't carry it by himself with only one arm."

Josie pulls a face. "My, my, we are getting domesticated, aren't we? Why can't Scott or Whistler do the shopping? I'd watch it if I were you. Those three will have you ironing their shirts and darning their socks if you're not careful."

She sounds so exactly like Tamsin having a go

at Becky that Tamsin thinks about it again on her way over to the flat. Jim would certainly want her to go and play badminton if that was what she preferred, but the fact is that she would rather spend the evening with him, going to Sainsbury's, cooking a meal, listening to music. Is that being dull and restricted, all the things she used to taunt Becky with? It doesn't feel like that; but then she has an inside view now.

As it turns out, there's no cosy twosomeness about the evening at all, because Glyn is there with Whistler and then Scott comes in with Louise, and they end up making a huge curry and sitting on the floor eating it, amidst the usual token expressions of guilt about unfinished essays and untouched reading lists.

Walking back rather late, Louise remarks, "I hope you're not going to back out of this Lake District trip next weekend just because Jim's crippled himself?"

Tamsin has almost forgotten about it. She tries not to give way to the feeling that she will be abandoning Jim at a low point: he won't be able to do any of the things he usually likes to do at weekends, but on the other hand he does have an enormous reading list to get through.

"You don't have to feel guilty," Louise says. "There's not much he can't do for himself somehow or other, and anyway Scott and Whistler will be around."

"It's all right, I'm not going to drop out. Jim

would never dream of missing a trip just for me, would he?"

"Nan's operation won't be until Easter," Abigail says on the phone, "so you can go off on your weekend without thinking there'll be an instant crisis. And it depends on the results of the tests anyway."

"So I'll probably be at home anyway when it happens."

"Yes. I don't know what your plans are for Easter," Abigail says more brightly, "but if you want to invite this accident-prone boyfriend of yours to stay for a few days I'm sure we could find room."

"Thanks," Tamsin says. "I'm not sure yet."

Jim is deep into Shakespeare's problem plays when she goes round on the Thursday evening before the Lake District weekend.

"What *are* problem plays, anyway?" she asks, looking at the heap of texts and literary criticism scattered across the sofa, with pages of notes in Jim's rapid slanting handwriting.

"Shovel it out of the way if you want to sit down." Jim is making one-armed coffee in the kitchen. "They're plays like *Measure for Measure* and *All's Well that Ends Well* and some critics say even *Hamlet*. Plays that can't be classified as either tragedy or comedy but have bits of both –"

"Like real life?"

"Well, sort of – plays that don't end neatly but leave some things unresolved or unsatisfactory –"

"Like real life again?"

"Ambiguous characters, so that you don't know whether to sympathise with them or not –"

"Sounds exactly like real life to me."

"As I was about to conclude – according to the learned Shakespearean scholar, Ms T. Fox, problem plays are exactly like life." Balancing a tray on one hand, Jim brings the coffee in and they sprawl on the floor as usual, leaving the books where they are.

"I've been thinking," Jim says.

"Oh yes?" Tamsin assumes an expression of extreme surprise.

"Yes, seriously. Listen. My brother's offered to sell me his old car fairly cheaply. It's an ancient rattletrap, but it starts and it stops and it goes, which is basically all you need in a car. I don't know one end of an engine from the other but you could tell me when to change the plugs or put oil in or whatever you have to do to cars. I can't really afford it, but as I can't go to the Alps now and I'd reckoned on paying for that, I might buy it."

"Can you drive?"

"Yes, I passed my test while I was still at school. Anyway, I thought a car might be useful for when I finish here. I was thinking we could go to Ireland in it in the summer –"

"You can't drive to Ireland. Haven't you noticed? There's the Irish Sea in the way –"

Jim raps her hand. "Will you listen, and take me seriously? – I know you've got your work in industry, but you'll have a few weeks off. Wouldn't you like to go to Ireland? You said you wanted to go back there. Dublin – the Wicklow Hills – the Ring of Kerry – we could go to Patrick Pearse's cottage, and to Yeats' grave under Ben Bulben – sure it'd be great, wouldn't it?" he finishes in his Cork accent.

"Mountains?" Tamsin says doubtfully.

"Of course. Slieve Bloom, McGillicuddy's Reeks, Carrauntuohill." Jim says the names as if offering her his most treasured possessions.

Tamsin knows what will happen if she tries to follow Jim up mountains. Yes, she does want to go to Ireland, she does want to be with Jim, she does love mountain scenery, but as a combination she is not at all sure that it will work.

"But you know I'm no good at mountains," she says.

"Nice rounded summits they have in Ireland, no problem at all. And the other reason I'd like to get a car is that I've been thinking about what happens after I leave here." He rolls over and props himself on his left elbow, carefully moving his right arm in its sling. "An English degree is practically useless in terms of getting a job, as my dad regularly points out, but I'll have to earn some money somehow. I've been thinking about a part-time course in journalism, but I've got to do something to pay off my loan. Even bricklaying –"

"But you haven't done an English degree to use it for bricklaying!"

"No, I know. I expect something will turn up, but the point is that whatever I end up doing I want to be near you."

"But, Jim," Tamsin protests, "this is your life, your job. You can't base it all on something so –"

Jim frowns. "So what? Unimportant? Trivial? Is that what you were going to say? Is that all this means to you?"

His tone is light, teasing, but with an undercurrent of seriousness. In the dim light his eyes are almost black, watching her steadily.

Tamsin hesitates. "So uncertain" was what she had been going to say. "No," she answers, "not trivial, of course not, but –"

"You wouldn't let it get in your way, you mean?"

"No, that's not what I mean at all!" She tries to explain. "It might not work, you and me – you shouldn't stake your career on it. You should do what you want to do, not what happens to turn up."

Jim is silent for a moment and then he says, "That's a big difference between you and me. Your career's going to be important to you. Mine's probably going to be a way of paying off my debts, keeping a roof over my head and earning enough to carry on doing the things I like doing. I don't even think in terms of a career."

Suddenly Tamsin realises why this makes her

uneasy: it is like her father. Not as he is now, but as he was when Abigail knew him. "Paul was never bothered about anything," Abigail told her. "Something will turn up, things will sort themselves out, why worry? That was his motto. And if he wasn't worried about anything, I felt I didn't have to worry either." Tamsin tries to weigh this up, deciding whether the attitude itself bothers her or whether it is purely the association with her father. Jim is not much given to worrying, it's true, and that makes his present mood seem out of character.

He prods her. "Hey! What are you thinking about?"

"That my father used to be just like that," she admits.

"Oh, thanks a lot," Jim says huffily. "Look, I meant what I said just now. I don't want to be in your way, if that's how it seems. You've got a lot going for you – you're bright, you're ambitious, you're beautiful, you know what you want to do, you're only in your first year and you're going to meet all sorts of people and have all sorts of chances. You'd be pretty damn stupid to throw it all away on an idle slob like me. I'm not going to be much use to you."

"Don't make me sound like some horrible calculating yuppie!"

Jim turns his face away. "I'm only being realistic. OK, you're not horrible and calculating, but no one could blame you for feeling like that."

"But I don't! And now who's saying it isn't going to work?" she accuses him. He has never spoken like this before and she is dismayed by it. Their precious evening together is dangerously close to ending in argument.

"I'm not saying that," Jim mumbles. "Only, if it's going to be finished as soon as I leave here, Goodbye Jim the day after the exams, I think I'd rather know now and start getting used to it. I don't want you to stick around out of charity, just because I've broken my arm and my finals are coming up."

"Jim! Stop it! Why are you talking like this?" She twines an arm around his neck. "You're crazy if you think that's the only reason I'm here now, out of *charity* – there are far worthier charities to support! I'm here because I want to be, because we – like each other and have fantastic times together and –"

He turns back towards her and rubs an unshaven cheek against hers, looking at her sidelong, suggestively. "Could be even better though."

"Yes?" she says, and then, understanding, "Aha! Is this an elaborate variation on *If you really cared, you'd sleep with me*? Is that what all this pathetic I'm-useless talk is for?"

"Not really," Jim says, but then he smiles and adds, "but partly. It's all right, I'm not propositioning you right now – this arm is a bit of an encumbrance. But it would be *nice*. And I'd prefer it if you didn't go stampeding off like a herd of wildebeeste when I suggest you might stay the night. It doesn't do a lot for my morale."

"I suppose Candida used to stay?" The words are out of Tamsin's mouth before she has formed the question in her head.

Jim draws back, offended. "What the hell has Candida got to do with it?"

"But did she?"

"Well, yes, she did. Does that matter?"

"No. Yes. I don't know."

I can't be feeling *jealous*, Tamsin tells herself: I won't. I'm a rational human being, an independent 1990s woman. It doesn't matter at all.

"Listen," Jim says, still frowning. "It was all over with Candida a long time ago, I've told you that. And it wasn't the same thing at all, though I don't suppose you'll believe me. It was no big deal to Candida; she's been going through men like library books ever since. When she came along ready and willing it would have taken a stronger character than me to resist – well, I was more than happy to oblige, until she found out I was only an Irish navvy. But that's irrelevant now – surely you can understand that?"

"Yes."

"Is that really what's bothering you?"

"No," Tamsin says. She takes a deep breath. "It's not Candida. It's not you. It's not even that I don't want to. It's a sort of daft superstition – that – that if I let myself get too involved with you,

I mean more than I already am, something awful will happen. It's a kind of family tradition. The other day, when I got the phone message – it seemed as if I'd been waiting for something like that to happen, for you to kill yourself climbing."

"But I didn't kill myself, did I?"

"No, but it's always going to be a possibility, isn't it? You only have to look at the mountain rescue statistics. I can't kid myself that the other Sunday is the only time I'm ever going to be worried about you – if we stay together. You're not going to the Alps now, but you will, and then there are all those Scottish mountains with the lovely names, and the Dolomites, the Pyrenees, the Peruvian Andes and God knows where else you'll think of going. I don't mean that I want you to *stop* – it's part of you, and you wouldn't be the same if you were happy sitting indoors watching television, but for me it's a . . . a dread, that's always going to be there. I can't help it."

Jim looks at her and then takes her hand and looks down at their entwined fingers.

"But I could just as easily have an accident walking across a harmless bit of floor – I've just proved that," he says. "Or falling downstairs or walking in front of a bus. *Life's* a risk. And about the climbing, I'm not exactly in the Chris Bonington league, as you seem to think. We take *more* care climbing than any other time, because we'd be stupid not to. I might as well decide that I'd better not get involved with you in case you fall off a bridge or electrocute yourself or get crushed by a JCB on one of your site visits."

"Well, it does sound silly, put like that –"

Jim looks at her in exasperation. "Why are you such a gloom-monger, idiot? Why do you automatically expect the worst? If I have a minor accident you assume I'm dead, if your mum goes out with a man you imagine her stabbed to death in an alleyway. On that basis you'd better avoid friendships and relationships for your whole life, because you never know what might happen to spoil them. I suppose, according to your theory that the worst must always happen, you think if you come to bed with me I'll get you pregnant and then clear off, because of this peculiar idea that I'm like your father. Well, let me assure you I've no intention of doing either. If you don't feel strongly enough then I shall have to put up with it, but if it's because you don't trust me, I'd prefer it if you did. Because you ought to. I suppose I should have mentioned before," Jim says belligerently, "that I love you. Perhaps you haven't realised, though I would have thought it was obvious."

"Jim, I –"

A key turns in the lock and both Tamsin and Jim turn abruptly to see Scott's smiling face in the doorway, with Louise behind him. "Hi! We've brought you some chips."

"Oh, bloody hell," Jim mutters into Tamsin's jumper.

Next evening Tamsin and Louise catch a train to Penrith and then a bus, arriving at Patterdale Youth Hostel to find the evening meal almost over. The party is a large one, consisting of women mainly in their twenties and thirties. It seems that these weekends occur regularly throughout the year and already there is a festive air of reunion. Tamsin and Louise sit down to the meal which has been saved for them, eat and clear up quickly, and listen as the plans for the two days' walks are outlined by Marianne, the small spiky-haired woman who has organised the weekend.

"Tomorrow, there's a choice of two routes to the summit of Helvellyn and then we're going to stay up on the ridge and come down via Dolly-waggon Pike and Grisedale Tarn. Those with a head for heights can go via Striding Edge. Those who'd prefer the easier way can go over Glenridding Common, which is a bit farther but not so airy. On Sunday, we're doing a picturesque low-level walk along the shores of Ullswater and coming back by boat."

Tamsin's heart dips at the mention of Striding Edge. She realises that a look at the map should have told her that Helvellyn would be very likely to feature on the programme, being so close to the hostel. And then it occurs to her that she is being given a chance to redeem her disgrace, to prove to herself that she can do it, that she doesn't have to give way to fear. Striding Edge has become her personal testing-ground.

She looks at Louise. "What do you think?"

Knowing what happened last time, Louise says tactfully, "Er . . . I don't know. I couldn't honestly claim to have a head for heights."

"I think I'd like to try," Tamsin says, although she knows that it won't be a question of trying: she must either decide to do it, or not. One thing she cannot do is dither about, like last time.

"It'll be all right if the weather's reasonable," says a friendly woman at their table, who wears parrot earrings and is appropriately called Polly. "I've been across Striding Edge before, on a fine day. If there's a strong wind I shall go the easier way."

"Let's wait till tomorrow and see what the weather's like," Louise demurs.

It was dusk when they arrived at Penrith, so next morning gives them their first glimpse of the fells. Excitement clutches at Tamsin's throat when she steps outside before breakfast. The day is bright, clear, spring-like, with a light breeze and scudding clouds. It's the sort of day that makes her worries seem foolish: Jim is right, she does always expect the worst, when there is probably no need to worry at all. Nan might not be seriously ill after all, Mum will be happy with Roger, Paul Strivener can't interfere with her life unless she chooses to let him. But there is one test she must set herself, now that the choice has been put to her: she must cross Striding Edge. She can't allow herself to take the easy option.

"Oh well, if you're sure," Louise says as they go up to the dining-room for breakfast. "If I'm terrified I shall blame you. I know Candida said there was nothing to it, but that's Candida."

"Candida," Tamsin says, "does seem to make light of things."

Louise gives her a suspicious look. "Are you doing this to prove something to Jim? Because if so, I don't really think you need worry."

Perhaps not. Tamsin thinks of her parting from Jim on Thursday night. "Phone me," he said, "won't you?" She said yes, of course she would, but now she senses that a lot depends on that phone call. First, she must get across Striding Edge, which stretches like a tightrope between them.

"It's more a case of proving something to myself," she says. "I'm never going to be a climber, but that doesn't matter. Jim can't swim."

Louise collects cereal from the serving-trolley. "You're joking! I thought everyone could swim."

"Well, Jim can't."

"OK, Striding Edge then. We can give each other moral support."

Tamsin sits down with her cornflakes and pours tea for Louise and herself. She is thinking of the first time she made herself jump from the high board at the swimming pool. She knew she would be scared, but nevertheless she made herself mount the steps and walk along the webbing surface of the board, beyond the hand-rail, to stand on the edge. It made her feel sick to look down but she forced herself to stand there, gripping the edge of the board with her toes. After minutes of dithering, fighting a desire to go tamely back down the steps, she made up her mind, closed her eyes and jumped. Air swooshed past her body, the water smacked and shocked her and closed over her head, the pressure hurting her ears. She opened her eyes in a swirl of bubbles and churned water, kicked up to the surface and filled her lungs with air and felt like shouting with joy. She can still remember the sense of achievement, not just because of having jumped but because of making herself do something that frightened her.

If she could jump from the high board at the age of eleven, she can cross Striding Edge now.

The clocks are going forward for summertime this weekend. Walking along the lane, Tamsin sees celandines growing in the damp soil under the trees and hears birds singing in the hawthorns; everything speaks of spring, life, optimism. At Grisedale Bridge they part company with the other group, which is going farther along the road before turning off for the more gradual approach to Helvellyn. Marianne's party takes the route

Tamsin walked before, the lung-bursting slog up to the Hole in the Wall. They make frequent pauses to get their breath back and look down at the valley to see how far they have climbed. The fells are pale green today, spring-washed, without the brackeny colours of last time; there is a faint sprinkling of snow on the highest ground.

Climbing the last rise before the slopes fall away at the start of Striding Edge, Tamsin feels the tension building up in her stomach, the first sparkings of fear. In half an hour it will be over: she will have done it, or not. She voices her new superstition to herself: if I do this, if I get to the summit, everything will be all right. I'll phone Jim as soon as we get down and tell him. We'll make plans together and I'll invite him home to meet Mum, and we'll go to Ireland . . . If I do this, I'm going to stop worrying and enjoy all the things I should be enjoying. And if not . . . I'll know I'm a coward, a giver-up and runner-away, like my father.

The scenery is opening out on both sides, dappled cloud-patterns, green valleys rising to blue ridges and peaks, but she isn't going to look at the views yet. Not until she's on the other side of the ridge; then she will allow herself the reward of looking down. The leaders of the group are moving out now in single file, along the crest ahead. Tamsin reaches the first broad slabs, tries to banish the sense of imminent panic and follows. The slopes of rock and scree veer away and her eyes try to follow the dizzy gradient, but she resists, determined not to look down and scare herself. Her stomach sways with the familiar sick feeling and her mind produces a quick slide-show of all the things that could go wrong: she could lose her balance, there could be a freak gust of wind, someone could come the other way and knock her off, she could grab a rock that isn't secure ... On the other hand, it's more than likely that none of those things will happen at all; why should they? She only has to think carefully about what she is doing. Her hands and feet move forward carefully, following the person in front. Behind her, Louise is making progress with little squeaks and gasps.

And then Tamsin comes to a standstill at the precise place that daunted her last time. She recognises the individual rocks, the jutting surfaces, the stretch that is just a bit too close to the steeper edge on her left. Her mind jibs at it, taking in the yawning drop below. But everyone in front of her has managed it, and there is no wind today to blow her off balance. "Make your mind up and do it," she remembers Jim saying, standing exactly here. "You've got to commit yourself."

I will!

She takes a breath, and moves decisively forward. A stretch, her hands reach forward, grabbing, her left foot wavers over empty air and then finds a firm hold, her body straightens. A slight teeter, another step and she is past the awkward point, looking at easy footholds in front of her. She resists the urge to yell out in triumph, because she isn't there, not yet. She turns round to see if Louise is all right and sees her hesitating, her face screwed tight in concentration.

"OK?"

"OK. Thanks," Louise gasps.

For a moment Tamsin allows herself to look down and enjoy the heady sensation of being up so high. It is more exhilarating than frightening. She is in control, capable; she is committing herself. The end of Striding Edge is in sight now, where the narrow ridge meets the main bulk of the mountain, marked by a knot of people in bright waterproofs. She looks up at the final part of the climb, the boulder-strewn rise to the summit, where she will soon be standing.